## UNHAPPY DISCOVERY

It was the man Slocum was looking for, all right, stuffed back against the closet wall, a knife stuck deep in his chest, his eyes looking grotesquely upwards, as if beseeching the Almighty to take him.

Slocum was just about to swear when he heard a noise that brought his head around.

He put a finger to his lips so that Chan wouldn't talk.

Slocum listened.

Gradually, in between the battering winds, he detected the sound of footsteps on the wooden interior stairs.

Somebody was coming up here.

He grabbed Chan by the hand and dragged him into the closet, reaching out and pulling the dead man inside too.

Slocum drew his gun.

They were about to have a visitor—the man was certain to find the blood all over the floor and get curious—and Slocum wanted to be ready to greet him properly.

The sonofabitch was really going to be surprised.

# DON'T MISS THESE
## ALL-ACTION WESTERN SERIES
### FROM THE BERKLEY PUBLISHING GROUP

**THE GUNSMITH by J. R. Roberts**
Clint Adams was a legend among lawmen, outlaws, and
ladies. They called him . . . the Gunsmith.

**LONGARM by Tabor Evans**
The popular long-running series about U.S. Deputy
Marshal Long—his life, his loves, his fight for justice.

**McMASTERS by Lee Morgan**
The blazing new series from the creators of Longarm.
When McMasters shoots, he shoots to kill. To his enemies,
he is the most dangerous man they have ever known.

**SLOCUM by Jake Logan**
Today's longest-running action Western. John Slocum rides
a deadly trail of hot blood and cold steel.

# JAKE LOGAN

# THE SILVER STALLION

JOVE BOOKS, NEW YORK

SLOCUM 197: THE SILVER STALLION

A Jove Book/published by arrangement with
the author

PRINTING HISTORY
Jove edition/July 1995

ISBN: 0-515-11654-8

A JOVE BOOK®
Jove Books are published by The Berkley Publishing Group,
200 Madison Avenue, New York, New York 10016.
JOVE and the "J" design are trademarks
belonging to Jove Publications, Inc.

PRINTED IN THE UNITED STATES OF AMERICA

10 9 8 7 6 5 4 3 2 1

# 1

A foggy night in San Francisco, too many drinks at a saloon situated on the wharf, and John Slocum found himself following a small but noisy group of men to a warehouse located nearby.

Slocum had only seen cockfights once before. He'd watched a few minutes and then left, disgusted at the pleasure the crowd took in the blood and pain of the combatants.

Maybe tonight would be different.

The warehouse was packed with various kinds of horse-drawn wagons in various stages of repair. The air smelled thickly of axle grease. In the middle of the dirt floor was a penned-off area where the battle was to take place.

Both cocks wore two-inch spurs, which were really doubled-edged razors attached to their legs. About a century ago a Mexican had apparently decided that there wasn't enough blood being spilled in the arena. So why not make sure there was a lot more.

The spurs were so cumbersome for the cocks that they sometimes cut themselves. Slocum had even heard of a cock that had accidentally cut its own throat.

Slocum stood watching as the fight began. The tension was starting to sober him up. In the pit, the cocks were being urged to fight.

The place was starting to get oppressive, with all the cigarette smoke and men yelling and the cocks starting to cut each other. Because this was the Barbary Coast, the roughest part of the entire Bay area, the place smelled of vomit and urine, the barn being used for any number of illegal activities by very drunken men.

He'd definitely made a mistake coming here.

He was just turning away from the pit when he sensed somebody watching him.

At first, glancing around at the open barn door and the bales of hay on both sides of the walls, he saw nobody.

But then he looked up to the catwalk and saw a man staring down at him. The man was definitely out of place here, what with his expensively cut Edwardian suit, bowler hat, and stylish walking stick.

The man continued to stare at him.

Slocum started to wonder if maybe some of the stories he'd heard about men in San Francisco might not be true. . . .

Slocum left the barn.

In the dark streets now, a chill midnight rain fell and fog, like ghostly tumbleweeds, rolled down the boardwalks.

Slocum was tired. He'd been in San Francisco two days, having responded to a telegram from a friend of his, Sam Myles, a former Pinkerton man who had once saved him from drowning after Slocum had been shot in the chest and then fallen into a swollen river.

The telegram had read:

WORKING ON CASE OF THE CENTURY STOP
REALLY NEED YOUR HELP STOP GET HERE
AS SOON AS POSSIBLE STOP

How could Slocum say no? He had packed his carpetbag, gone down to the Kansas City train depot, and set off for the Bay area.

There was only one problem. When he'd reached Myles's office, he'd found the door locked, the lights out, and a San Francisco police detective lurking at the opposite end of the hallway.

"I'm looking for Sam Myles," Slocum had explained after the dour man had flashed his badge.

"So are we," the detective had replied. "For first-degree murder."

Slocum had been here two days now and the only place he'd seen Myles was on the front page of the newspaper.

Wanted for murder. A $2000 reward for any information leading to his arrest. Armed and dangerous. Be very cautious.

Footsteps behind him.

Coming closer. Faster.

Ever since he'd visited Sam's office, Slocum had felt that someone was following him. He thought of the dapper man in the hayloft tonight. Was that his tail?

And who was walking behind him now in the fog?

Slocum reached a corner and paused. Half a block ahead was the kind of seedy tavern known as a deadfall. Only the oldest and weariest of whores plied these places; only the cheapest rotgut was served. Robberies were never reported, nor were most murders. San Francisco cops were generally afraid to work the Barbary Coast, and when they came down here it was generally in twos and fours, armed with shotguns and bats.

Slocum decided to have a quick beer in the deadfall ahead. Maybe he could get a glimpse of the person behind him.

The smells of the place almost gagged him. On the dance floor, accompanied by a concertina, three couples held each other and danced. One of the women had her hand inside her partner's pants, giving him a hand job. The guy looked unconscious. The men were sailors, the women aged whores who likely carried diseases. San Francisco was going through a plague of venereal diseases that was starting to claim six lives a day according to the newspapers.

A serving woman, one shorn of teeth and a right arm, came up and took his order for a glass of beer.

He stood next to the window, peering out into the night.

A few minutes later, his dapper friend from the cockfight appeared, walking intently, looking frustrated that he had lost Slocum somewhere.

In moments, like someone entering the netherworld, the man and his dapper bowler and his even more dapper walking stick vanished into the fog.

Who was he? Why was he following Slocum?

"There are some nice women here tonight," the serving woman said when she brought his beer.

"So I noticed."

"You arrogant fuck," she said, catching his sarcasm. "Think you're better than we are, don't ya?"

Slocum felt sorry for the woman, and even sorrier that he'd been flip with her. These women had enough grief in their lives without his sarcasm.

"You're right. I shouldn't have said that."

He took a greenback and laid it on her serving tray.

Then he headed for the door.

He enjoyed the chill rain. It smelled clean and fresh. Helped get rid of the deadfall's smells.

He was tempted to catch up with the dapper man and start following him.

But he hadn't slept well the last few nights. He needed some good, nourishing shut-eye.

Anyway, he was sure the man would find him again tomorrow and resume his surveillance.

Slocum went on into the night, leaving the Barbary Coast section of the city twenty minutes later, finding his way to his inexpensive but respectable hotel not far from the business district.

Less than twenty minutes after that, he was in his room with the lights out and the covers pulled up under his chin. He was going to sleep tonight. No doubt about it . . .

He was just starting to dream, when the window off the fire escape was pried up and a dark figure with a gun walked over to his bed and started to shake him.

"Slocum. Slocum. Wake up."

# 2

Five minutes later, Slocum sat on the edge of his bed, having climbed into his trousers and managed to build himself a cigarette in the gritty glow of the oil lamp on the bureau.

He shared a pint bottle of bourbon that his friend Sam Myles had brought along.

Myles didn't look so good. After taking off a fake beard and a massive greatcoat, Myles looked chunky and tired. Dark rings curved beneath his eyes. His dark suit was wrinkled and threadbare.

But Myles was always one for a good front. He was a dreamer who rarely let reality get in his way.

"You ever seen one hundred thousand dollars in greenbacks?"

"Guess I haven't, Sam."

"Well, you're going to. And very soon now."

Slocum puffed on his cigarette. "Sam, can I be honest?"

"Hell, yes."

"You look for shit."

"Well, hey, pal, nice to see you too."

"What I mean is, you look like you're in trouble."

It had been trouble of various kinds, usually involving the lethal combination of women and money, that had gotten Sam Myles kicked out of the U.S. Army, a brokerage house he'd worked for, and finally the Pinkertons. Pinkerton himself had caught Sam trying to shake down one of his clients.

Slocum had no illusions about his friend, but what could he do—the man had saved his life.

Myles smiled. "I know what you think about me, pally. You think I'm a crook."

"Sam, I—"

"No, no. That doesn't bother me. Because I am a crook. Or was. Past tense."

"Then this new thing . . ."

Sam Myles leaned forward like a carnival huckster spotting a fresh mark. He even held up his hand as if he were about to take an oath on a bible.

"I swear to God, John, this time it's legit. You want to hear about it?"

"Sure."

Myles glanced at the window. "You mind if I pull that paper shade down?"

"Be my guest."

Myles got up and walked to the window. "They're after me, John. They want me dead. That's why they put this phony murder rap on me."

"You didn't kill anybody?"

Myles grinned. "Not the guy they said I did. They killed him and set me up for it. But once I get this cleared up . . . there isn't anything much sweeter than holding one hundred thousand dollars in your hands."

"Is one hundred thousand dollars worth losing your life?"

Myles pulled the shade down and turned back to John. "How about one hundred thousand dollars and a chance to be a genuine hero? A chance to make up for an entire lifetime of fuckups and con jobs on people you actually cared about?"

Slocum grinned. Sam Myles was something to see when he got himself up and rolling like a fire-and-brimstone minister. "What the hell did you hook yourself into, boy?" Slocum asked.

Myles came back, sat down, and took another sample of the bourbon.

After handing the bottle to Slocum, he said, "Good government."

"Afraid you've lost me."

"Hell, John, you've only been here a couple of days, but you should already have caught on to the fact that everybody from the mayor straight on down to the lowliest copper on the beat is crooked. On the take."

Slocum laughed. "Let's just say that I strongly suspected they weren't virgins."

"Well, there's a small group of very prominent people in this city who want to clean everything up—from the crooked mayor on down."

"And they've hired you?"

Myles shook his head. "Not in the way you think." He smiled. "For once, I had some good luck, John. One night I was doing some surveillance on this very prominent banker—his wife hired me to see what the old boy was up to—when I met this beautiful young woman named Eve McKay who was running from a couple of real bad guys. They were trying to beat her up. I got her out of there."

"That's good luck?"

"Let me finish." He took a drag of his cigarette.

"The woman's name is Eve McKay. You want to know who beat her up?"

"Who?"

"The mayor himself. Seems she had some ledgers of his that could tie him to all the local corruption."

Myles was about to say more when a knock fell suddenly upon the door. He put a *shushing* finger to his lips.

Myles glanced around the room in panic and then nodded to the closet.

He tiptoed over there, silently opened the door, and silently put himself inside.

"Who is it?" Slocum said.

"Police."

"I'm trying to sleep."

"You open the door, asshole, or I'll put you to sleep for a real long time."

Sighing, Slocum got up from the bed, padded across the floor on his bare feet, and opened the door.

It was the same cop who'd questioned him the day he'd gone up to Sam's office.

"Remember me, cowboy?"

"Unfortunately, yes."

"Detective Halliwell."

He came into the room and looked around, a tall, thickset man with red curly hair that was just starting to turn gray.

"Where is he?"

"Who?"

"Guy you were talking to. I was out in the hallway. I heard him."

"You didn't hear anybody in here. Maybe I was talking in my sleep."

Halliwell walked around the room and ended up at

the window. He pulled up the shade and looked out. As his eyes swept the city below, Halliwell said, "What's your part in all this, Slocum? You another cheap chiseler like your friend Myles?"

"Myles is all right. No better or no worse than most of us."

"You sound like a minister."

"Maybe I missed my calling."

Halliwell turned back to him. "What is your calling anyway?"

"Drifter."

"Figured."

He started walking toward the bureau, on the right side of which was the closet door.

Halliwell tried to make it look casual, but Slocum could see what was coming.

Halliwell drew his Smith & Wesson service revolver, threw open the closet door, and lunged inside.

"Get out here, you sonofabitch," Halliwell said.

Slocum expected to see Sam Myles come out, arms held over his head.

"You hear me, you bastard?" Halliwell said.

A silent half minute went by.

Halliwell came out of the closet. "Where is he?"

Slocum almost laughed. That fucking Sam Myles. Sometimes he was a magician. Where the hell had he gone to anyway?

"I told you I was alone in here."

"Bullshit."

"Well, Halliwell, you checked the closet yourself."

Angry, Halliwell went over to the bed, got down on one knee, and looked beneath the bed.

"Shit," he said.

"I hate to see a man of the law get frustrated this way," Slocum said.

On his feet again, Halliwell put his face close to Slocum's and let him have a little hot sour whiskey breath. "I'm going to nail you both, Slocum, and when I do you're going to stay nailed. Right up until the day they hang you."

"I was in my bed asleep," Slocum said innocently. "I just don't know what you're talking about."

Halliwell went over to the hall door and opened it. A drunk wandered past, wobbling down the hall.

"You're a punk, Slocum, just the way your friend Myles is a punk. You think you're smart and you think you're lucky, but you're going to learn that you're not either one."

He wasn't angry when he said this, only weary. There was even a hint of sadness in his voice.

"That's all I see anymore on this job, Slocum, punks like you and Myles. Punks who do exactly what they want until their luck runs out."

He shook his head, walked out, and closed the door quietly behind him.

Slocum locked the door so Halliwell couldn't come charging back in. Then he heard the closet door squeak open.

Sam Myles appeared. He was smiling. He tiptoed over and said, "Did I fool that bastard Halliwell or what?" He had the good sense to whisper. Halliwell was probably right outside the door. "Fooled that sonofabitch, didn't I?"

"Where were you?"

"Little trunk up on the shelf. Squeezed my fat ass into it." He leaned closer. "I'm leaving now, kiddo. I'll be back in touch with you tomorrow. I'm going to need your help.''

''Be careful, Sam. Don't do anything crazier than usual.''

''I'm going to be a genuine hero, pally. It's going to give me a whole new start in life. A new man.''

Myles went over and slipped his beard and greatcoat back on.

He waved and went over to the window, edging it up gently so it wouldn't make any noise. The fog had rolled away. The night was dark and chill.

He had the window about halfway up when the rifle shots cracked through the outside darkness.

Slocum was already moving toward the window when Myles screamed and fell over backwards.

# 3

Two bullets had exploded into Sam Myles's chest and now the man, blood bubbling from his mouth, lay quickly dying.

"Damn, John, I won't get to be a hero after all." He tried a smile, but the blood ruined the effect.

Slocum knelt next to him. "You'll make it, Sam. Just relax for now."

"C'mon now, John, we never bullshitted each other before. Let's not start now."

Pounding on the door. "It's Detective Halliwell, Slocum. Open up in there."

More pounding.

People in the hallway.

Feet shuffling; whispering.

Myles's eyes were starting to roll back into his head. He took Slocum's hand and grasped it.

"John, in my office . . . my desk. Taped to the bottom of the second drawer . . ."

He gasped. Sucked down blood. Coughed. His whole body was trembling.

"Go right now. Get it before the coppers do . . ."

He died. Nothing dramatic. The light gone from his eyes, lips suddenly slack, big hand limp in Slocum's grasp.

Pounding again. "You open up in there, Slocum!"

Slocum leaned over and drew Sam Myles's eyelids down.

A minute later, he had turned down the lamp and was in his clothes, huddled down beneath the window.

The sniper who had killed Sam was probably still out there, eager to take another shot or two.

Slocum eased himself to his feet, standing by the side of the window.

He leaned over, pushed the window up as far as it would go, and then walked back by the bed.

Only one way he had even a chance of making it.

"Slocum!" Halliwell shouted, then slammed his shoulder against the door.

Slocum ran toward the window and dove through it, much as he'd dived into the old swimming pool as a boy.

He hit the fire-escape landing in a ball, unrolled himself, and began running down the fire-escape stairs to the alley.

The shots came immediately, *spanging* off the iron of the fire-escape stairs.

Slocum stumbled once, but grabbed the railing to keep from pitching down the steps.

He reached the alley sweaty, out of breath, and deeply pissed.

He was now out of rifle range.

He hurried through the night to Sam Myles's office.

Because the entrance doors were locked, Slocum was forced to go around back and use his modest skills as a lock-pick. He'd once helped out a guy nicknamed "Fingers," and in return Mr. Fingers had been nice enough to teach Slocum how to get past virtually any lock with but a single small burglary tool.

Slocum got inside in less than ten seconds, mounted the back stairs in the shadowy building, found the third floor, and went into Sam's office.

He decided against lighting a lamp.

Faint moonlight outlined a large desk, two chairs, a wooden filing cabinet, and a small bookcase overloaded with folders and papers.

He took a step toward the desk.

Wood creaked.

His own footsteps?

In the eerie darkness, only the chill night winds could be heard, rattling windows, sending weather vanes into delirium.

Another step toward the desk.

Wood once again creaking.

But somehow—perhaps because the creaking sound came a little bit late—he knew now that he wasn't alone in the office.

He drew his .45.

"I'm in the mood to blow somebody's ass away," he said, his voice ragged and mean in the darkness. "You've got five seconds to show yourself. Then I start shooting."

The wind again.

Faint sounds of San Francisco night, including a distant tugboat.

"Now you've got three seconds."

His finger started to get eager on the trigger.

"Two."

"No, please, don't shoot!"

He had expected anything—man or woman; angry or scared—but he had not expected this.

He turned slowly around and pointed his .45 at the deep shadows falling to the right of the filing cabinet.

"Did you hear me, mister?"

"I heard you. Get over here by the window so I can see you."

"You're scarin' me, mister."

"Just do what I tell you."

But the edge had already gone from his voice and his .45 was already lowering in his hand.

She was pretty much like most of the other homeless kids Slocum had seen on the streets, especially near the Barbary Coast.

She was dressed in a dirty work shirt a few sizes too big, a pair of boy's brown corduroy pants that were pretty much worn through, and a cheap pair of Western boots of the kind city folk wore. Even though her hair was cut short, her natural beauty was plain to see. She was maybe twelve.

"Who're you?" Slocum asked.

"I have every right to be here," she said.

"Oh, yeah?"

"Yeah. This is my father's office."

"Your fath . . ." He stopped. "What's your name?"

"Lilly."

"Lilly what?"

"I'm called Lilly Thane but that's not my real name. My real name's Lilly Myles."

"And your father is—"

"Sam. Sam Myles. He's a private investigator."

"Aw, shit," Slocum said.

She laughed. "You said a dirty word."

"Sam really had a kid?"

"Uh-huh. Me."

"And he knew about you?"

Silence.

"He knew about you?" Slocum repeated.

"No. But he was going to. That's why I came up here today. To see him. To tell him. My mom died of consumption last week and told me all about him right before she passed on. Took me all week to find him. I snuck in here tonight when the colored man who does the cleaning came in. Thought I'd just wait here till morning and surprise him."

Slocum sighed, shoved his .45 back in his holster, walked a couple of steps to the chair behind the desk, and sat down.

"You all right, mister?"

"Yeah."

"What's wrong, then?"

"I'm thinking."

"About what?"

"About how I'm going to tell you about your dad."

"Aw, shit," she said.

"Who told you you could swear? You're a very pretty little girl. Don't go ruining it with a dirty mouth."

"I just said it because you did."

"Well, then I'll just have to start watchin' my language around you, won't I?"

"He's dead, ain't he?"

" 'Isn't' he. 'Ain't' isn't a word."

"You didn't answer my question, mister."

"My name's Slocum."

"Slocum, then. You didn't answer my question. He's dead, isn't he?"

"Yes, he is." Silence. "You all right?"

"I don't want to say anything right now."

"All right."

She took two steps to the window and looked out at the night sky.

"You know what she did?" the girl said after a time, her back to Slocum.

"Who?"

"My mom."

"No, what did she do?"

"She was a whore."

"Oh."

"And she didn't die of consumption. She died of venereal disease. They put her in an insane asylum. And she had these sores all over her body. I—I'm ashamed to say this, but by the end, when I'd go up there to visit her, I was afraid to even touch her. And she was my own mom."

"I'm sorry, Lilly."

"And then I thought that I'd come and live with my dad and . . ."

She started crying gently, little more than a silhouette against the moonlit window, a sweet little girl with a whole passel of adult griefs.

He went over and brought her gently back to his chair, and sat her in his lap and put her head on his shoulder and then let her cry her ass off.

She seemed to have a lot stored up.

In the meantime, he leaned forward, eased out the proper desk drawer, and found the key taped to the bottom. He also took a small address book.

She cried for a real long time, with him passing her his handkerchief every few seconds, then finally just giving her the damned thing to keep.

"You going to find who killed him?" she said when her tears had trailed off into sniffles.

"Yes, I am."

"Nobody should've killed my dad."

"No, they shouldn't have."

"He was going to take care of me."

"Yes, he was."

"We were going to live in a fine big house together and be very happy."

"Yes, you were."

"I'll bet he was a nice man."

"He sure was. He was a hero."

"Really? My dad was a hero?"

"He certainly was."

She put her face back to his shoulder and started crying again, but this time softer.

"You promise you'll find who killed him?"

"I promise."

"Solemn word, Slocum?"

"Solemn word."

After a while, Lilly went back to the window. Dawn was a pearl-pink color. Slocum came over and stood behind her. Below them was a small square on all four sides of which sat a variety of businesses, including everything from a haberdashery to a bank with a statue of a horse on its front walk, from a bookstore with the name SHAKESPEARE across its front to a dress shop for women, the mannequins in its front windows looking eerily real in the dawn light.

"You hungry?" he asked.

She nodded.

"How does bacon and eggs and toast sound to you?"

"Sounds great. As long as coffee goes with it."

"Coffee? You'll stunt your growth."

"That's an old wives' tale, Slocum. You know what an old wives' tale is?"

"Yes, believe it or not, even dumb old Slocum knows what an old wives' tale is."

She laughed. "Good, then you're not as stupid as you look."

"Thank you, Lord, I've passed her test."

"You know what I mean, Slocum. You just look like this big, dumb cowboy. No offense."

"Of course not. I like hearing myself being described that way."

"That's all I mean, Slocum, that you're not half as stupid as you look."

They locked up the office, went down the back stairs, and out into the cold but invigorating morning.

"Was my dad really a hero?"

"Yes, he was."

"God," she said proudly. "That's really great. A hero. I guess my mom didn't know that about him. Otherwise she would have told me, don't you think?"

He reached down and ruffled her hair. "Sure she would've, kiddo. If she'd known about it, I mean."

# 4

After breakfast, which cost him nearly four dollars, and during which he witnessed young Lilly cleaning off three plates of food, Slocum found the young girl a hotel for her to stay in.

After installing her in Room 405, he lectured her about keeping the door locked at all times, and he invented a four-tap knock as a code so she'd know it was him.

"This is like Nick Carter," she said.

"Yeah, I suppose it is."

"Except he's better-looking than you are."

"Thanks."

"And he smells better."

He laughed. "Well, your highness, I haven't had a chance to take a bath yet today. And for what it's worth, you don't smell all that good yourself."

She blushed. "I really don't?"

He gave her a squeeze. "Yeah, you do. I was just being petty and thought I'd pay you back."

"Aw, thank God. For a minute I was afraid you were serious." She looked up at him and shook her head.

"But you know something, Slocum?"

"What?"

"You really do stink."

"Appreciate the sentiment."

He went to the door. "Keep it locked."

"I know. But I still think you should leave me a gun."

He looked around the drab but clean room. There were some yellowbacks on a corner table. "You just sit here and read and don't worry about guns."

"Slocum?"

"Yeah."

"You don't smell bad. I just like to see you get frustrated. I mean, it's kind of funny. This big tough cowboy who lets a little girl get under his skin and all."

He nodded good-bye and grinned. "You don't need a gun anyway, Lilly."

"How come?"

"You've always got your mouth."


As he entered his own hotel, he noticed again the young woman who had smiled at him every time he passed through the lobby. Strawberry blond of hair, sumptuous of body in her blue silk dress, and highly seductive with her big blue gaze, this time she winked at Slocum and then proceeded to move quickly to the staircase.

She went up to the third floor. He was close behind. Given all the things that had happened, he needed some kind of release. And this was about the best kind of release there was.

She went into 304 and closed the door.

He went up and knocked. The door was not closed. It yawned open.

He went in, closing the door behind him.

The blonde was over by her bureau, brushing her long hair.

She was naked.

"I didn't think anybody could undress that fast," Slocum said.

"I can when I want to."

"And you wanted to?"

"Very much."

"I'm flattered."

"You should be. I usually charge twenty-five dollars for this."

"That's a lot of money."

"I'm worth it."

Slocum grinned. "I'll bet you are."

She came into his arms then, and while they were kissing, she skillfully unbuttoned his trousers and slipped out his swollen cock.

"A nice big one. Yummy," she said between kisses.

She gently pushed him back on the bed, stroking his cock while kissing his now-naked chest and nipples. She worked her way down until she was right up against the swollen head of his cock, and then she began to run her tongue up and down its length, fondling his testicles at the same time.

John moaned, and the woman finally took him in her mouth and began to work on him expertly. . . .

After a violent explosion of passion that made him temporarily blind, he decided to return the favor by using his own tongue, running it over the random sprinkling of freckles, and then he started to lick inside her, cupping the cheeks of her ass so he could lift her off the bed while he gobbled her up.

Then he was finally inside her, and the bed was groaning and singing, and she was starting to scream, in exultant pleasure and gratitude for having a cock this big and this hard and this relentless filling her up and turning pleasure into a heady mix far stronger than opium. . . .

"You're really something, you know that?" she said later.

But he was too modest to say that he'd been told that often in his travels. He simply got dressed, said, "Thank you, ma'am," and left.

Forty-five minutes later, he stood in his hotel room after bathing and changing clothes, packing his carpetbag.

All the way up the stairs, the manager had whined about Sam Myles getting killed in the hotel. "We are a very elite place," the man had said. Slocum had decided not to hurt the man's feelings by answering that boast.

He finished packing and went over and stood over the spot where Sam Myles had died.

Scrubbed blood still stained the linoleum. The window was still shattered from bullets.

Poor Sam.

Maybe he had been going to go completely straight after all. Maybe he had even been going to be a real hero.

Too bad he hadn't lived long enough to meet Lilly. Maybe the girl would have changed him too, turned him into a proud and dutiful parent.

A knock. Slocum glanced up, right hand falling to his holstered .45. "Who is it?"

"You know who it is."

Detective Halliwell.

"I don't want to talk," Slocum said.

"Ever stop to think that maybe I don't give a shit what you want? Now open up."

Slocum opened up.

Detective Halliwell came in and walked around with the air of a very confident man. "You'll get it next," he said.

"Oh?"

"Sure," Halliwell told him. "Because they figure you've got it."

"I don't know who 'they' is and I don't have any idea what 'it' refers to."

"How long you going to keep on playing the yokel?"

"As long as necessary."

Halliwell, in his dark suit and bowler, went over to the bloodstained spot and touched the blunt toe of his black shoe to it.

"He was scum, Slocum. Just in case you're getting sentimental on him, I mean."

"Maybe I knew a different man than you did."

"You want to see his police record?"

"You mourn your dead, Detective Halliwell, and I'll mourn mine."

Halliwell took out a small black cigar, bit off the end, spat it on the floor, took out a stick match, dragged it across the top of the bureau, and got his cigar going.

"You beat me to his office," Halliwell said.

"Did I?"

"They're going to kill you for what you've got, Slocum. One side or the other'll kill you and take it from you."

"I still don't know what you're talking about."

Halliwell walked over to the window and looked out. "Never seen a body of water as beautiful as the Bay."

Slocum just listened.

"My family goes back three generations here. Love this place. Every one of us. Just one problem with it." Halliwell flicked ashes on the floor. "Crooked government. Been that way almost from the start. If we could just get some honest people in there . . .''

Halliwell was silent for a time, watching a schooner arc across the horizon line.

''You could change it all, Slocum.''

''I could, huh?''

Halliwell nodded. ''Wouldn't it make you feel good to do something clean and decent for once in your life?''

Slocum said nothing.

''He told you something, Myles did, before he died, didn't he? Something about city government. He had something on them—that's why they killed him. You won't know what to do with it anyway, Slocum, so why not just turn it over to me?''

Slocum wanted to get going. He said, ''I'll think it over.''

''There isn't much time. They'll be watching you, just waiting for their chance, the way they did with your friend Myles.''

Slocum went over, picked up his carpetbag, and started for the door.

He took a final look at the bloodstained floor. ''You're full of shit about Sam Myles, Detective Halliwell.''

''I am, huh?''

''Yeah,'' Slocum said, glaring at him. ''He made a lot of mistakes but he was basically a decent guy.''

''Probably went to church every Sunday, didn't he?''

''Anybody ever tell you you're a prick?''

''Yeah, my mom did when I was six years old.''

''Remind me to buy your mother a drink,'' Slocum said.

The two men left the room and went down the stairs to the lobby, where several old man sat in oversize chairs playing Parcheesi and reading old newspapers.

Slocum paid his bill and walked out into the sunlight.

"They're probably watching you right now," Halli-well said.

"Got me in their gunsights?"

"Exactly."

"How do I know you're not a crooked cop working for the mayor?"

A curious mixture of anger and sorrow appeared in Halliwell's hard gray eyes. "My younger brother was also a copper. Undercover. Trying to prove how corrupt the mayor was. They found out and killed him. He left four kids and a wife."

"I'm sorry," Slocum said.

"Yeah," Halliwell said, walking away, "you should be."

Slocum had walked two blocks when he ducked quickly around a corner and peeked back at the sidewalk he'd just been on.

There, in all his splendiferous glory, was his tail from last night, the dapper man with bowler and walking stick.

# 5

Gamblers, thieves, harlots, and crooked politicians—along with a variety of other parasites—had come to San Francisco back in the Gold Rush days and had never left. They began to ply their various trades in an area that stretched from the East Street waterfront all the way to Chinatown. The neighborhood was soon dubbed the Barbary Coast.

Daylight did it no favors.

Slocum stood on a hill looking down at the crowded streets of cheap clothing stores, pawnshops, gambling dens, bawdy houses, and restaurants that made up most of the Coast.

In the sunlight, you could see how old and ugly and filthy the area was. Same for the people. By the time they were ten or eleven, it was said, some of the hookers, female and male alike, had slept with so many johns that they looked four times their age. One bawdy house openly advertised its eight-year-old whores.

The police reckoned there were four murders, one hundred robberies, and fifty serious beatings a night.

This did not include men being drugged and drunked

up and being "crimped" by boardinghouse owners who "sold" the men to ship captains in need of sailors.

It was into all this that Slocum now descended, wishing he could leave San Francisco and get back into the clean fresh air of the American West, which was where he really belonged.

The smells were the worst part.

Garbage, with fat eager rats, was everywhere, overflowing cans that lined the sidewalks, heaped in piles out in front of small shops.

The narrow, curving streets were so much alike that Slocum soon found himself lost.

He stopped a Chinese man and asked him for directions.

The Chinese man, apparently under the impression that anybody as clean and intelligent-looking as Slocum must be an undercover copper, shook his head and rushed away.

Finally, Slocum found an elderly hooker who was wobbling drunkenly down the street. In the daylight, her heavy makeup gave her the look of an old and very sad circus clown.

"I'm looking for Davis Street."

She winked. "That's where they keep the young ones."

"Can you help me?"

She winked again. "My pussy may be a little old but it's smart. I taught her how to do tricks those little girls will never figure out."

"Right now I just need to find Davis Street."

She shook her head. "Little cunts. Someday somebody's gonna start killin' 'em. They took all my business away."

"Davis Street, ma'am," Slocum said. Talking to a drunk was a mighty frustrating business. "Can you help me?"

"Want a hand job?"

"No, thanks."

"Blow job? It's good 'cause I ain't got no teeth."

Giving up, he turned and started walking away.

"Hey."

He turned back to her.

"Davis Street. Three blocks down and to your right. Then one more block and to your left."

"I appreciate it."

"I've got a real smart pussy here, my friend."

"I'll keep that in mind."

Davis Street was no different from the other streets surrounding it, a long shabby line of joy houses and saloons and pawnshops. The smells of rotting garbage and human sickness weren't any better either.

There was a man lying on the sidewalk having some sort of seizure. Slocum was about to help him when two Chinese hookers appeared and dragged him back into the saloon. Apparently, the guy still had a few dollars left; otherwise they would have left him outside.

The address he wanted was a small two-story frame house with a HOTEL sign out front.

Slocum went inside.

The front room had been turned into a small office where an old white-haired man with a too-large blue glass eye stared at him. His other eye was brown. "You be wantin' a room?"

Slocum shook his head. "Looking for somebody."

"Oh?" The old man, who wore a faded and frayed suit coat and a badly wrinkled white shirt beneath, was suspicious immediately. In a place like the Barbary Coast, you distrusted anybody who asked questions.

"A woman named Eve McKay."

"Never heard of her."

"I'm told she lived here for a time."

"Well, young fella, whoever told you that was wrong."

Slocum looked around.

A staircase to the right led to the upstairs. Down the steps now came a very drunk whore and a very drunk sailor. Their weight was heavy on the old wood. They both grinned in the direction of the old man.

"You know what day it turned out to be, Charlie?" the hooker said.

"No, Cherine, what day did it turn out to be?"

"It's his birthday."

"Well, I'll be."

"I told him in that case, I'd give him a free one."

"That's damned white of you," old Charlie said.

She giggled. "Yeah, that's what I told him. That it was damned white of me, I mean."

They left.

"She looked a little young," Slocum said.

"Hell, she's twelve," Charlie said.

"God, a regular grandmother."

Old Charlie looked at him with his glass eye. It was too big for its socket and looked as if it could be plucked out with little trouble. "I take it you ain't from around here?"

"Just visiting," Slocum said.

"You keep on the way you are, you're ain't never gonna make it out of here alive. I'm tellin' you that for your own good."

"Asking questions, you mean?"

"Exactly."

"Eve McKay. She's my cousin."

"Oh?"

"Yeah. I had to come to California, so I thought I'd look her up."

"Your cousin, huh?"

Slocum nodded.

"She worth a lot of money?" old Charlie said.

Slocum smiled. "Maybe you heard of her, huh?"

"Maybe."

Slocum reached in his pocket and pulled out some greenbacks. He slid two of the bills across the registration counter, and glanced at the registration book. "Looks like you've got a convention going on here."

"Convention?"

"Yeah. A 'John Smith' convention. Must be a dozen of them registered here."

Old Charlie smiled sourly. "Kind of a smart aleck, aren't you?"

"Kind of, I guess." Slocum nodded to the greenbacks on the counter. "When do I see Eve McKay?"

"When do you want to see her?"

"As soon as I can."

"I'd need two hours."

"That'd be fine. Where?"

"You know where the Salvation Army is over on Montgomery Street?"

"I can find it."

"There's a saloon half a block away. Fat Amy's."

"Sounds charming."

"You're being a smart aleck again."

"Guess I am."

"She'll be there, Eve will." Old Charlie scooped up

the greenbacks and put them in his pocket. "You always been a smart aleck?"

"Pretty much, I guess."

"That kinda shit don't go over too good down here."

"It doesn't, huh?"

Old Charlie jabbed at his eye with his thumb. "That's how I got this."

"Yeah?"

Old Charlie nodded. "Seen a guy in a saloon who walked just like a duck. You couldn't help but notice. Kept walkin' past me all night, so finally I couldn't help myself—you know how you get when you're drunk—he walked past this one time and I just started quacking. You know, like a duck."

"And he didn't like it, huh?"

"Didn't like it? You know what I found out later? Earlier that night he'd walked in on his old lady screwing this big black colored guy. You know how pissed off a guy would be about that? Just about anything would set him off. Especially somebody quacking at him."

"I imagine."

"So when I quacked at him, he just went crazy. The thing was, he was about half my size too. I mean, I just figured I'd hit him a few times and that'd be that." He shook his head. "But the sonofabitch was crazy. And I mean literally. So this is what I got for quacking at him."

"The glass eye?"

"Yeah, and one ball that never quits hurting."

"I'll never quack at anybody ever again," Slocum said. "I promise."

"See," old Charlie said. "I just tell you my quacking

story—trying to give you a little friendly advice—and there you go again."

"There I go again?"

"Sure. There you go again being a smart aleck."

"Oh," Slocum said, turning toward the door. "I guess I was at that, wasn't I?"

He got out of there before old Charlie could tell him any more stories.

# 6

In her time, Lilly had slept in alleys, bathtubs, haylofts, wagon beds, and hotel hallways. When your mother was a whore and dragged you along wherever she went, you never knew where you might sleep.

And you developed a keen sense of hearing.

Like other small, vulnerable animals, sleeping children were subject to all kinds of predators.

So you had to be ready to move, and move quickly, and you had to be ready to defend yourself.

Soon after Slocum left, Lilly Myles crawled up on the big, comfortable double-size bed and promptly went to sleep.

It had been a long time since she'd slept in a room this clean and nice and safe.

She went to sleep quickly and slept without jerking awake to any of her usual nightmares.

Lilly was disoriented when she woke up. Where was she? How had she gotten here? What was she doing here? Then she remembered.

John Slocum. Her father's friend. Her father's office.

All her tears. All her pain. And Slocum bringing her here after agreeing to find the man who killed her father.

Lilly yawned, curious as to why she'd awakened. The sky was still blue in the window. She couldn't have been asleep that long. So why had she awakened?

And then, lying there, toasty warm from sleep, stretching long and lazy like a cat in summer sunlight . . . she heard it.

In the hallway. Footsteps. Whoever it was, was heavy enough to make the wood of the hallway floor protest.

Slowly, Lilly sat up in bed.

She tried to be sensible. Maybe she was imagining things. Her mom had always said that. How Lilly let herself get carried away.

Maybe a heavyset man was walking down the hallway to his room. Maybe the footsteps were nothing more sinister than that.

Silence.

She sat alert, like an animal with its ears turned back, scanning an area for suspicious sound.

Silence. No movement at all.

See, Lilly? See, that's all it was, some heavyset guy going to his room. And here you were getting all upset and—

The doorknob turned. She wouldn't have seen it or heard it if she hadn't been so wide awake. Whoever was turning the knob was doing it with a lot of skill and finesse.

Shit, she could just hear him whispering to himself. Locked.

She eased herself off the bed. Damn Slocum anyway. She'd told him she needed a gun. Now look at the spot she was in.

She paused. Listened. The doorknob no longer

moved. The silence again. What was the guy up to any?

A faint scratching. Metal against metal. What was he doing?

It took her a few seconds to figure it out. Some kind of burglary tool. The asshole.

Lilly had once watched a guy named Wienie pick a lock this way. He'd done it real fast, then stepped back and went da-da like he was a magician or something. That's what this asshole was doing. Picking the lock. It probably wouldn't take him more than a few seconds.

Aw, shit. She heard the lock open. He'd be in here right away.

She glanced around the room. Damn Slocum anyway. She'd told him to leave her a gun.

And then she heard the door start to squeak open. And heavy footsteps made the hallway floor squeal again.

Damn Slocum anyway.

# 7

After leaving the small frame house that called itself a hotel, Slocum walked a quarter block down the busy street and stood beneath the overhang of a Chinese restaurant.

He built himself a cigarette and settled into doing some waiting. Patience had never been one of his virtues. He was much happier taking action.

Soon a young Chinese man left the hotel holding a note. He quickly hurried away. Charlie, the white-haired man with the glass eye, emerged fifteen minutes later. He had some kind of carrying case in his right hand.

He walked down the street toward Slocum, who stepped back even farther into the shadows.

"If you give me a penny, I won't tell him you're watching him."

Slocum looked into the darkened entrance of the restaurant. There was a Chinese kid, who could be no older than eight or nine, puffing on a cigarette and watching Slocum.

"A penny, huh? That's a lot of money."

"Otherwise I'll tell."

"How do you know who I'm looking at?"

"The man in the white hair walking toward us. As

soon as he got on the street, you took three steps back to hide yourself.''

''Very observant.''

Slocum flipped the kid a penny. He also wanted to give him a lecture on blackmailing. The stakes should be a lot higher than a penny.

But there wasn't time for a lecture. Charlie was moving quickly.

Slocum waited until the man had walked past him. Then he fell into step a quarter block behind him.

The streets were packed with people of every color, costume, and temper hurrying on into the chilly but sunny day. Shop owners shouted bargains at passersby; hookers offered lewd smiles; pickpockets descended on the elderly with ugly fervor.

Despite his age, Charlie rolled right along, deftly weaving his way in and out of the knots of people cluttering the sidewalk.

A few blocks north, he took a right, heading toward the wharf, the carrying case swinging heavily in his hand.

The smells changed here, Chinese cooking giving way to the bloodier and greasier tastes of American cooking.

At the wharf, Charlie turned left. There was a large, crumbling warehouse at the end of the block, one that had probably been built when the first seamen got here fifty years ago.

Charlie walked up to the first-floor door, took out a key, and let himself inside.

Slocum stood a quarter block away, watching. Better to give Charlie a little time to get inside and about his business. If he was busy, he wouldn't be so apt to hear Slocum sneaking up the stairs.

Slocum felt something jab his back.

When he turned around, his eyes level, he saw nothing.

"Hey. Down here."

The same little Chinese boy who had pestered him earlier was pestering him again. In the daylight, the kid looked a lot scruffier, his red shirt and corduroy trousers heavily patched.

"Kid, look, I'm really busy. I don't have time for games."

"No games. I help you."

"Help me?"

The kid put out his hand, palm up. "A penny please."

"I already gave you a penny."

"Another penny, please."

Sighing, still keeping an eye on the warehouse, Slocum dug into his pocket and brought out a penny. "Here you go. Now get the hell out of here."

"Vital information."

"Huh?"

"For this penny, I will give you vital information."

"Yeah, and what would that be?"

"A half a block away is a man. He has been following you all the time since my uncle's restaurant."

"Yeah? What's he wearing?"

The kid told him.

Slocum grinned, and mussed the kid's hair. "I didn't mean to snap at you, kid. I've just got a lot of things on my mind." He flipped him three pennies. "You catch good. Now go buy yourself some licorice or something."

"But the man following you . . ."

"I'll take care of him, all right?"

The kid had tears in his eyes suddenly. "I lied."

"About what?"

"About that place being my uncle's restaurant."

"It isn't?"

The kid shook his head. "I don't got no uncle. I live in an orphanage."

"Aw, shit, kid, this isn't the right time for this kind of thing—all right?"

Slocum felt like an asshole sending the kid away, but what could he do? He had to get inside that warehouse and find out just who Charlie really was and just what bearing he had on Sam Myles's murder.

Slocum flipped the kid a nickel. "How's that?"

But this time the kid didn't smile. The tears standing in his eyes wouldn't let him.

He just soberly dropped the nickel into his pocket, turned, and walked slowly away.

Great, Slocum thought. Now I get to feel like a cold-hearted sonofabitch all day.

Just before he went to the warehouse, Slocum decided to surprise Bowler Hat by turning around suddenly and running after him. Slocum wanted to find out who this guy was and what he wanted.

But Bowler Hat must have anticipated the move because when Slocum turned around—Bowler Hat was gone.

He gave Charlie five more minutes. Then he moved, down the street, around to the back of the warehouse, up the stairs leading to the windows on the second floor.

He stared through a spiderwebbed pane of glass into an empty office, everything inside covered with dust, the floor a minefield of dried rat turds.

He put his ear to the shattered window and listened.

No sound.

Charlie must be somewhere in the center of the building. Ordinary sounds from there would have a difficult time reaching the window.

Maybe there was a big office in the middle of the second floor. With a door that could be closed.

Maybe Charlie was sitting in a place like that. So it wasn't going to do Slocum any good to stand outside all day, the beautiful Bay behind him, his skin starting to gooseflesh from the cold winds.

He spent the next four minutes taking the window out of its casement. He used his trusty pocketknife and a considerable litany of profanity to get the job done. He leaned the smashed window and frame against the wall, then climbed into the building.

Everything had that high corrosive smell of rat shit.

He eased his .45 from his holster, and walked on the toes of his boots to the door of the small office he was in.

He opened the door an inch at a time, then peeked out. The hallway was lined with abandoned office furniture that now had a silver patina thanks to all the cobwebbing and dust covering it.

He listened. No sounds except for the aches and moans of a building this old, the creaks of rafters, the whistles of a half-toppled chimney.

Where the hell was Charlie?

He opened the door wide enough to sneak out into the hallway.

He noticed that his heart was beating a little faster. His grip tightened on his gun.

He went all the way down the hall, all the way to the front of the building, peeking into offices. You could see where tramps had slept here, building small fires to do a little cooking, piling up paper to fashion a mattress.

You could also see where females of various types had come to birth their young on wintry nights. A couple of gnarled white forms were infants that had not lived long. The ants had had at them and they were nearly unrecognizable.

But mostly what Slocum paid attention to was the silence. Strange. He was sure he would have heard Charlie leave, was sure he would have—

Slocum spun around, crouched, .45 ready to fire. There had been a sudden noise behind him, footsteps on the ancient boards. He looked down the long, dusty hallway that was shadowy even at midday.

No sign of anybody.

He looked at all the office doors. Of course there could easily be somebody hiding in one of the offices. He hadn't checked the closets. Somebody could . . .

He decided maybe he was imagining it. This place gave him the creeps. Maybe he just thought he'd heard—

"Hi."

Slocum's little Chinese friend stepped out from behind a door, trying hard as hell to look winsome so Slocum wouldn't kick his ass around the block.

"Aw, shit," Slocum said.

"You say that a lot."

"What the hell're you doing up here?"

The kid started looking teary again. "I just wanted to help you. I didn't want anything bad to happen to you. I just wanted to tell you what I found."

"What's your name?"

"Chan."

Slocum calmed himself. "Chan, I want you to give me your word that you're going to turn around and go back the way you came and get out of this building. All right?"

"But don't you want me to tell you what I found?"

"Whatever you're going to say, I want you to leave.

Right now. And don't come back. Understand?''

Chan shrugged. "I guess I just thought you'd be interested."

He turned away then, making a big sad show of his leaving.

He was playing with Slocum's mind, of course, and Slocum knew it.

The little bastard just wanted Slocum to say, "All right, tell me what you found."

But Slocum wasn't going to give him the satisfaction. No, sir.

He was going to get the little kid to leave, and then he could get back to his adult job of finding Charlie and his carrying case.

Slocum watched the kid shuffle down the hall, back toward the window.

Good riddance.

Slocum had started to turn back to the opposite end of the building when he decided that the little bastard had gotten him going after all.

"Chan?"

Chan whipped around eagerly. "Yes?"

"Why don't you tell me?"

"Tell me what?"

"You know, what you found. I mean, did you really find something?"

"Do you think I'd lie?"

Of course I think you'd lie, you little urchin, Slocum thought. But he said, "No, you're a very honest kid."

"And I'd make somebody a great son."

"Aw, shit."

"See, there you said it again."

"Goddammit, Chan, will you just tell me what you found?"

"I found Charlie. The old guy with the white hair?"

"You found Charlie? Where?"

"In the closet where I was hiding so you wouldn't hear me. At first I didn't even know he was in there, but . . ."

But Slocum wasn't up for any more talking.

He reached the urchin in four long strides, grabbed his shoulder, and said, "You show me Charlie."

Chan gulped, nodded, and led the way back down the hallway to an office near the window.

Slocum hadn't checked the closets because he'd figured Charlie was meeting somebody—and who would meet anybody in a closet?

Chan led the way into a dusty office, opened the closet door, and said, "Charlie."

It was Charlie, all right, stuffed back against the closet wall, a knife stuck deep into his chest, his glass eye looking grotesquely upwards, as if beseeching the Almighty to take him.

Needless to say, the carrying case was gone.

Slocum was just about to swear when he heard a noise that brought his head around.

He put a finger to his lips so that Chan wouldn't talk. Slocum listened.

At first, he didn't hear anything. Then, gradually, in between the battering winds, he detected the sound of footsteps on the wooden interior stairs.

Somebody was coming up here.

He grabbed Chan by the hand and dragged him into the closet, reaching out and pulling dead Charlie inside too.

Slocum drew his gun.

They were about to have a visitor—the man was certain to find the blood all over the floor and get curious—and Slocum wanted to be ready to greet him properly.

The sonofabitch was really going to be surprised.

# 8

Lilly just had time to jump up on the bureau and pick up a vase before the guy who'd picked the lock came into the room.

When the door swung back, it hid part of the bureau, which struck Lilly as a particularly good stroke of fortune.

The guy would come in, sneak a look ahead, sneak a look left, sneak a look right, but before he ever saw her she'd have time to—

And she did too.

Raised the cheap blue chipped ceramic vase, hurled it at the back of his head, and then watched as the fat florid man in a drummer's checkered suit went sprawling on the bed, his gun flying out of his hand, hitting the floor, and skidding over against the wall.

Lilly saw just what she needed to do. With no hesitation at all, she dove from the bureau and landed right next to the gun.

Meanwhile, the fat lock-pick was shaking his head and trying to regain some composure before he lifted his considerable self off the bed and then tried to get his hands on her.

But he was too dumb, too slow, and too unimaginative.

Sure, she might look like a dumb little kid, but she was anything but.

She grabbed his Navy Colt, jumped to her feet, and then raced over to where he was just pushing himself up from the mattress.

She put the business end of the gun right against his ear. ''What's your name?''

''I'm gonna whip your ass.''

''I'm holding the gun and you're going to whip my ass? You're as dumb as you look.''

She pulled the hammer back. The sound was loud enough to fill the room.

''Hey,'' he said. ''You be careful of that gun, little girl.''

''Next time you call me 'little girl,' I shoot you. You understand?''

''Uh-huh.''

''So what's your name?''

He told her.

''And who do you work for?''

''I can't tell you that.''

''Sure you can.''

''They'd kill me.''

''Well, if you don't tell me, *I'll* kill you.''

''Are you a midget or something?''

''One.''

''Huh?''

''Two.''

''What're you doing?''

"Counting to five. If you don't tell me by then, I'll kill you. Four."

"What happened to three?"

"Four-and-a-half."

"Hey, wait a minute!"

So he told her who he was working for.

And that was when she said, "This is for calling me 'little girl,' you fat stupid bastard."

And then brought the gun down hard across the back of his skull.

This time when he hit the bed, he didn't get up.

# 9

Slocum eased the hammer back on his .45 and peered out through the crack in the doorway.

He still couldn't see anybody, though the footsteps were getting closer, heavier.

"I have to go to the bathroom," Chan whispered.

"You'll just have to hold it," Slocum whispered back.

And then he saw him.

Dark suit. White boiled shirt. Celluloid collar. Dark hat. And the indispensable sawed-off shotgun.

Detective Halliwell paused in the office doorway and looked down at the blood on the floor. His eyes followed the smears of blood from the floor into the closet.

He raised his eyes and fixed them on the closet door.

He brought back the hammer on the sawed-off shotgun.

"If I were you, I'd come out of there," Halliwell said. "With your hands over your head."

"You think he'll let me go to the bathroom?" Chan whispered.

Slocum frowned, stuffing his gun into his holster. He

eased the closet door open with the toe of his Texas boot. "We're coming out," he said. "Easy with that shotgun."

"Why, if it isn't my good friend Mr. Slocum. Somehow I'm not surprised."

"You heard what I said about the shotgun, Detective Halliwell."

Slocum stepped out into the light, Chan right behind.

"You have a new partner, I see," Halliwell said.

"He adopted me."

"Are you really a detective?" Chan asked Halliwell.

"Uh-huh."

"Dedicated to upholding the law equally for all citizens, the way it says in Nick Carter?"

"I forgot to mention he's a con artist," Slocum said to Halliwell. "Hold on to your wallet."

"I need to pee, Mr. Detective," Chan said.

Halliwell frowned, then nodded to the hall. "Go out there and do your stuff and then get back in here."

"Yessir."

Chan left.

"Who's the kid?"

"He latched on to me while I was doing a little surveillance work."

Halliwell shook his head. "Poor little bastards. The streets full of orphans these days. I'd like to take him home to the missus." He frowned. "Lost our only child when he was six to rheumatic fever."

Slocum said, "You're not holding up your end of the bargain."

"Oh?"

"You're supposed to be this ruthless, corrupt cop who's trying to stop the truth from coming out. It's not fair if you start taking in orphans."

"I want to nail the mayor's balls to the wall. Maybe someday you'll believe that, Slocum, and help me."

"Help you how?"

Halliwell indicated Charlie's body propped inside the closet. "Don't shit a shitter, Slocum. Old Charlie there has been hiding Eve McKay for the past month and a half. That's why I was so hostile the first time I met you. I figured you were some gunny working for the mayor. Eve McKay knows where your friend Myles stashed the ledgers of the mayor's, the ones that show how corrupt he really is."

Slocum shrugged. "If that's really true, you should have seen that Myles was on the right side for once."

"Maybe, maybe not. The way I figure a guy like your friend Myles, in the end he caves in and sells the ledgers to the highest bidder, which in this case would have been the mayor."

"Maybe Sam changed."

"Maybe. But it's doubtful."

Chan was back. "Boy, do I feel a whole lot better." He looked at Slocum. "Now I'm ready to go and do some more detecting."

Slocum smiled. "I think I've got a better deal for you somewhere else."

"Huh?"

"Detective Halliwell there told me that he'd like to take you home for the night and have his wife give you a nice big meal."

Halliwell started to protest, then stopped himself. "Tuesday's stew night. Guess there's plenty of that to go around."

"Then I want you to tell Detective Halliwell all about yourself, all right?"

Chan shrugged. "He won't make me go to school, will he?"

"I don't think so."

"I hate school. It's boring."

Detective Halliwell leaned down and said, "Do you suppose you could keep quiet long enough for Slocum and me to finish our talk?"

Chan smiled. "Sure. For a penny."

"A penny," Halliwell said, digging in his trouser pocket, coming up with a small copper disc, and flipping it to Chan. "I see what you mean, Slocum, about him being a con artist."

Slocum laughed. "You're catching on fast."

Halliwell looked at the closet. "I've been keeping an eye on old Charlie for the past couple weeks. He always used this warehouse to meet the people who are hiding Eve so the mayor can't get his hands on her. I came up here to check on him and . . . well, I get the sense the mayor's closing in."

"Can you put more men on the case, really start looking for Eve McKay?"

Halliwell shook his head. "Most of the department is on the take. Which means it works for the mayor. I'm pretty much of a lone gun, I'm afraid."

Slocum mentioned the rendezvous point where he was supposed to meet Eve McKay at three o'clock. "I'll go there and let you know what I find."

"Be careful. That's tong territory."

"Tong?"

"Chinese gangsters. They make white gangsters look like altar boys."

"Wish I had that shotgun of yours."

Halliwell laughed. "I have to admit it comes in

handy, especially when I have to go to the Barbary Coast to arrest somebody.''

Halliwell looked down at Chan. "I'm not going to talk to you about school just yet.''

"Great!''

"But I am going to talk to you about getting a bath.''

"Oh, no, really?''

"And getting your hair trimmed.''

Chan frowned.

"And getting you some clothes without quite so many patches in them.''

Chan looked up at Slocum. "Am I going to prison?''

"You're too young to be a wiseacre.''

"No, I'm not," Chan said.

"He's all yours," Slocum said.

Halliwell said, "I'll get some men up here to take care of the body." He took a card from his vest pocket. "Here's where I live. In case I'm not at the station house.''

"Thanks.''

Halliwell led Chan from the room.

Slocum stared at old Charlie, propped just inside the open closet door.

First Sam and now Charlie.

The mayor seemed to be just as ruthless as Slocum had always heard.

# 10

Over the years she had had many names but now, in this time, this place, this city, her name was Belle Kelly.

"Miss Kelly?"

The colored maid had knocked softly. Now she stuck her head inside.

Belle lay in the center of a vast bed covered with silk sheets and topped with a matching silk canopy. The large, elegantly appointed room was as dark as dusk.

"Your friend is here, miss."

Belle swore. "I've told him never to come without giving me proper notice."

"I'm sorry, miss. He's here."

"Tell him he'll have to wait."

At age thirty-six, beauty was becoming a battle. True, with proper diet, exercise, and some small luck her classically beautiful face would always be just that—beautiful. But still, she needed at least an hour in front of her makeup mirror to fully effect the glamour that had claimed so many male victims over the years.

And now he was here without any notice at all.

The bastard.

It was as if he wanted to deny her power over him by seeing her without the mask of her beauty.

Bastard.

Twenty minutes later, her long blue dressing gown trailing behind her like a train, her gorgeous red hair tumbling down her shoulders, her eyes and lips perfectly made up to emphasize their erotic qualities, she entered the drawing room where Mayor Henry Carvelle waited, ever the gentleman in his elegant dark suit and silk top hat.

She watched his eyes carefully, judging the effect she had on him.

In his gaze, she saw desire and joy and just a little bit of fear.

Exactly what she wanted to see.

"Some coffee, perhaps, Henry?"

"No, thank you, darling. I'm already late to a meeting. I just . . ." His handsome face grew tight. "My friends asked me to ask you one more time if you wouldn't . . . reconsider."

"Oh, God, Henry, do you know how tired I am of talking about this?"

"I know. And so am I. But you know how important it is to all of us."

"I have no idea where she is."

"That isn't the point, Belle, and you know it. You could get her here in no time. If you really wanted to, I mean."

She laughed. "I think you're overestimating my powers, darling. It's true that I run the nicest house in all of San Francisco—with the loveliest and cleanest young flesh available—but that doesn't mean I'm good at tracking down missing persons."

Henry Carvelle cleared his throat. What he was about to say was difficult, even dangerous to a woman as volatile as Belle.

"You could send her a note and tell her the truth about who you really are, Belle. She'd come in a minute if she ever realized what your real relationship is."

Henry Carvelle's parents had come to San Francisco about the time of the first Gold Rush. They quickly realized that only fools and dreamers spent their time picking away in the hills. They managed to borrow a small amount of cash from their parents, both sets of whom were modestly successful merchants, and opened the city's first fashionable haberdashery. They made a great deal of money quickly, but unfortunately were unable to teach their son anything about success in business. He had been blessed with looks, charm, and a certain low cunning, but not with brains. Like most people who find themselves in this predicament, he went into politics, rising to a place on the city council. After that, after he was bought by the leading local gang, he became mayor.

He had served four years thus far. Another election would be coming up soon. There was no real chance he could lose. The reform movement, such as it was, had recently suffered a bitter split, so there was no formidable organized opposition to Henry and his people.

The only thing that could stop him was public disclosure of his ledgers.

"You're asking me to betray my own daughter," Belle said.

The words still seemed odd to her. Her own daughter. She had kept this secret from Eve all these years, pretending instead to be her aunt. Now Henry was asking her to tell the truth—as a way of luring Eve back home . . . and with Eve the ledgers.

"She wouldn't have those ledgers if it wasn't for you," Henry said.

She smiled. "That's so like you, Henry. Blaming me."

"To refresh your memory, my dear, I brought those ledgers up here one weekend to work. How did I know that your daughter would start poking through them . . . and sneak them off to her boyfriend, that stupid god-damned private investigator Sam Myles."

As she listened to him speak, a terrible realization came over Belle.

Much as he might lust after her, much as he might be afraid of her in some respects, he was absolutely willing to use her ruthlessly to get those ledgers back.

He said, "They've given me twenty-four hours."

"Who has?"

"You know damned well who has. The mob."

"Or what?"

He smiled sadly. "Or they kill me."

"Kill the mayor? Even they wouldn't be so stupid."

"You don't know them very well, Belle. They're not like the thugs you knew when you were coming up in New Orleans and Chicago. These men will kill anybody if they feel they need to. Anybody." He walked over to the window, a dandy of a boy-man who would never be tough enough for the world of real men. All he had was his daddy's money and reputation.

He looked out the window at fashionable Waverly Place and the neat black carriages that flitted by.

"I need the ledgers, Belle."

"Maybe there's another way to get her up here."

He turned back from the window. "She'll think it's a trap I put you up to—unless you tell her you're her mother. Then she'll want to see you right away."

Belle sighed. "You promise she won't be hurt?"

"She won't be touched. I give you my word."

"I'd kill you with my own hands, Henry, if anything ever happened to her."

"I'm not that kind of man, Belle. You know that. She'll be perfectly safe." He raised his hand and indicated the den where she kept her desk. "You could go in there now and write her a note. Have one of the people you know from the Barbary Coast get it to her—they'll know somebody who knows where she's hiding."

Ire showed in her dark eyes now. "You're not much of a man, Henry. And now I know you never will be."

He was about to protest her words, but she left the room too quickly, silk rustling as she moved with erotic grace.

She went into the den and closed the door.

A few moments later, she sat down, picked up a pen, and wrote a note to her daughter Eve.

# 11

The main occupation on Montgomery Street seemed to be puking.

Slocum had gone there to see if Eve McKay—who had no doubt been informed about their three o'clock meeting by now, probably by the young Chinese runner old Charlie had dispatched with a note—would actually show up at Fat Amy's.

So here was Slocum, twenty minutes early, walking down the narrow, filthy street trying not only to step over sleeping bodies, but also work his way around heaps of raw garbage.

And the vomiters weren't making his passage any easier.

If he didn't know better, being the cynical sort he was, Slocum might have thought that what he was seeing was nothing less than Montgomery Street's Salute to Puking.

Black, red, yellow, white, people of every color stood on the sidewalk, in the street, at the head of the alley, in doorways, and even leaned out of second-floor windows vomiting.

Finally, Slocum stopped a tiny Chinese man and said,

"What the hell's going on here anyway?"

"Wine. Bad lot." He shook his head sorrowfully.

"So they got sick?"

"Very sick," said the tiny Chinese.

And then he splashed some puke right on the sidewalk between himself and Slocum.

"Same to you," Slocum said, and wandered off looking for Fat Amy's.


He didn't know if she was Amy, but she sure was fat, whoever she was.

She sat in the dank, dark deadfall, up on the tiny stage, playing a piano while struggling to keep her enormous breasts from leaking out of her low-cut gown. Even in the shadows, her makeup had a lurid look, as if she'd been made up by an overeager mortician. The ditty she sang complemented her makeup perfectly. The words "pussy" and "cock" appeared frequently in the lyrics.

Slocum ordered a beer and stood at the bar.

"You here for the boar?" said the drunk next to him.

"Boar?"

"Yeah." The drunk nodded to the fat lady. "That's Helene."

"Ah," said Slocum, "the lovely Helene."

"She's the one that fucks the boar."

"Boy, I can't wait to see that." Slocum had heard of that, women screwing every kind of animal imaginable to keep the Barbary Coast customers happy.

Ah, romance.

"Fucker's got a cock on him like this. And between us, I think Helene kind of likes it."

"Well, thanks for the tip, friend. I'll be sure to bring the whole family. Something the kiddies shouldn't miss."

The drunk gave him an odd look. Obviously he sensed something wrong with Slocum's attitude, but he wasn't sure what.

The next time the bartender, who had nearly as many tattoos as scabs on his arms, walked by, Slocum said, "I'm supposed to meet Eve McKay here at three o'clock."

The bartender hadn't even been slowing down. But at the mention of Eve McKay's name, he turned and looked at Slocum and said, "I never heard of her." He was carrying a tray of glasses and a washcloth.

"Bullshit."

"You want me to set down these here glasses and break a fuckin' bat over yer head?"

"No. I just want you to tell me where I can find Eve McKay."

"I already told you, asshole. I never heard of no Eve McKay."

This had been a frustrating day for Slocum, so he probably went at the bartender a little harder than he should have.

His two hands lashed out, grabbed the man by the front of his shirt, lifted him up, and hurled him into the wall.

The man must have broken six, seven bottles of rotgut liquor when he collided with the wall. Not to mention all the glasses he'd been carrying.

The deadfall went ominously silent.

The lovely Helene even gave up her piano concerto.

"No reason for me to hurt you again, friend," Slocum said, "as long as you give me an honest answer."

The bartender started the long and embarrassing process of picking himself up from the floor and standing up again, like any other self-respecting human being.

"Play, Helene," he shouted to the hefty songbird.
She played.

"Talk," he said to two of the drunks at the bar.

"Helene gonna fuck the boar tonight?" one drunk
said to the other.

"God, I sure hope so," said his friend. "Been what?
Two, three nights now?"

"She gets a little sore from what I hear."

The first drunk grinned without teeth. "Bet that boar's
gettin' horny as hell by now, huh?"

They giggled.

Slocum was just about to say something to the bartender again when he felt a small, delicate hand slide
around his hip.

"Hi."

"Hi. My name's Kirstin."

"My name's Slocum. I'm looking for Eve McKay."

He got the standard Barbary Coast reply. "Never
heard of her, but I've got something you might want to
see."

Slocum nodded to the bartender. "He a friend of
yours?"

"He's a pig."

"Good."

There were three different beaded doorways in the
walls. He followed the voluptuous young lady through
the second one.

She didn't wait long.

Slocum had just rattled the beads by passing through
when she stood up on tiptoes and started kissing him,
sliding her tongue into his mouth.

"You ever do it standing up?" she said.

"Couple times."

"You like it?"

He smiled. "You really hate the bartender?"

"Yeah. I do. I only work here 'cause he promised to help me find my little sister. He's got connections. But I don't want to fuck none of the guys he brings here. But you . . ." She smiled. "You I want to fuck. I wanna get you up inside me and ride you like a stud. That sound good?"

What the hell, Slocum thought. There were worse fates than fucking a girl so she could piss off a bully bartender.

He started unbuttoning her clinging black dress, her bountiful breasts falling out, bouncing with youth, and took her left nipple in his mouth as he continued to take her dress off. He got his finger up her hot wet pussy and felt her hips begin to grind against his. He slid his hand around behind her buttocks and lifted her up so he could bring her full down on the hard lance of his cock. And then she really went to work, grasping his buttocks hard so she could grind his cock up deeper inside her. And then they found a heady breathless rhythm that had them both panting and making little animal mewls of blinding pleasure. They began to French-kiss so frantically that their heads snapped back and forth. He started grinding his way home then, finding her clitoris with his thumb and gently working it until she started coming so hard that he felt her go totally limp in his arms. And then he rode her home, as she virtually jumped up and down on the throbbing spear of his manhood. After he came, she eased him out of her, and then slipped to her knees and took the last searing molecules of his jism. When Slocum came, he went absolutely fucking blind crazy for about twenty seconds, and then he slumped against the wall, spent for another half minute or so. "Now that's what I call a friendly greeting," he finally said.

She smiled. "Just be sure to tell that asshole that I did it with you for free."

"You kept your part of the bargain. Now I'll keep mine."

Slocum went back to the bar and said, "She was great. And she didn't cost a cent."

"Fucking pig," the bartender said.

Slocum grabbed him again. "Now we're going to talk about Eve McKay, right?"

The bartender, not wanting to get hit again, led Slocum to the rear.

The deadfall was one big room with a small dance floor and tables taking up most of the space.

A man and his whore were passed out on the floor.

The bartender gave the man a savage kick when he passed by. "You owe me a fuckin' dime, Clete. You know you can't use this place as a roost. You think this is a dive'r somethin'?"

Gosh, Slocum thought, I sure don't see how anybody could confuse a place like this with a dive.

The bartender led the way through the beaded curtains.

Slocum followed.

The one with the ball bat got him first.

The one with the brass knuckles waited his turn.

The ball bat got him first across the back of the neck and across the shoulders, then right across the flat of the stomach.

Slocum immediately started to sag to the floor, but the one with the brass knucks had run out of patience and was putting deep and bloody grooves in Slocum's flesh even before his knees touched the floor.

Then they both started on him, and man, they whaled. Whaled every bit as much as the lovely Helene did when she was all dressed up for a special evening and really pounding those ivories.

And these were two boys who had really had a lot of practice at whaling too.

"Who sent you?" Ball Bat said while cracking Slocum across the knees.

"Fucking faggot mayor sent you, didn't he?" Brass Knucks said, putting a few more grooves in Slocum's shoulders.

All Slocum could think of was the Montgomery Street Salute to Puking because that was just what he was about to do.

"Aw, shit," Brass Knucks said when Slocum really started puking, "and I just cleaned them fuckin' boots of mine last month too."

# 12

The first pain he noticed was in his head. Tender to touch, tender even when Slocum moved it a half inch or so. The second pain he noticed was in his shoulders. The way the ball bat had been slammed against him, no wonder.

"You want more of the same thing?"

Slocum really couldn't see. Only hear. It was the voice of the bartender.

Slocum managed to get one eye opened. He was in some kind of cellar. The floor was damp and dirty. The walls were swollen with moisture. The stench was of a coffin opened after many years.

"You heard me, Slocum."

But all Slocum could manage to say was, "Water."

"Fuck water. You don't get any water till you tell me about the Silver Stallion."

"The what?"

"You know what—the Silver Stallion."

"I don't know what you're talking about."

The toe of a swift boot. In the ribs.

Slocum had been lying down on his side. Now he struggled to sit up.

"You going to whip my ass, cowboy? That what you got in mind? Well, I still owe you one for the way you threw me around upstairs. And believe me, I'm gonna pay you back too."

"Water," Slocum said.

Behind the bartender, an elderly female voice said, "Give him water."

"Since when are you the boss?"

"Give him water." The voice was obstinate.

"Shit," the bartender said. He reached over to where a glass sat on a chair, and brought the glass to Slocum's mouth.

Slocum raised a trembling hand and took the glass and opened his bruised lips.

They must have hit him on virtually every part of his body with either the bat or the brass knuckles.

He drank, the water chill and nourishing.

Then he closed his eyes, leaning his painful head back against the wall. He savored the water as it worked its way down into his stomach.

He knew momentary peace—no ball bat, no brass knucks, nobody pushing questions at him—questions that made no sense. The Silver Stallion? What the hell was that all about?

"You're working for the mayor, aren't you?" the bartender said.

"No."

"Where are the ledgers?"

"I don't know."

"Bullshit. Why are you so interested in Eve McKay?"

"Sam Myles told me about her."

"What about her?"

"None of your business."

The swift boot again. This time to Slocum's chest. He moaned and started to slump over again.

"Why are you so interested in Eve McKay?"

Slocum said nothing.

"Huh? Why?"

This time it was a slap, an arcing one that caught Slocum on the face. His nose started to bleed.

"That's enough, Gil." The woman again.

Slocum couldn't quite make her out. Parts of his vision were still murky.

"Like I said, since when are you the boss?" Gil said. Then, back to Slocum. "You want me to hit you again?"

"No."

"Then tell me about Eve McKay."

Slocum slowly shook his head.

There was a rustle of a dress. Tiny footsteps. A woman's voice: "Let me talk to him."

"Coddle him, you mean."

"Well, you've been beating him for quite a while now, and where has it gotten you?"

Gil sighed and stood up.

The woman sat down across from Slocum. She looked at him out of an ancient face with eyes that bore at least a hint of humanity and sympathy.

"I'm sorry they've been so rough on you."

Slocum said nothing.

"It's very important that we find out who you are and why you want to find Eve McKay."

Slocum said nothing.

Gil said, "Oh, yeah, this is working like a fucking charm. No doubt about it."

"Be quiet, Gil," the old woman said. Back to Slocum. "What's your name?"

Nothing.

"I'd like to know your name, please."

"John Slocum."

"Who do you work for?"

"Nobody."

"Not the mayor?"

"No."

"You mentioned Sam Myles. You knew him?"

"Yes."

"He was a friend?"

"Yes."

"Did he tell you about the ledgers?"

"Yes."

"Do you know where they are?"

"No."

"Bullshit," Gil said.

Slocum looked up at him. "If I had them, why would I be here looking for them?"

The old woman smiled. It was easy to see that she had been a real beauty in her younger days—even without makeup, in a drab gray, ill-fitting dress. "That's what I told Gil, but he wouldn't listen."

"Could I have more water?"

"Of course."

Gil said, "Why don't you just fix him a fucking steak while you're at it."

"Here you go," the old woman said, bringing the glass to Slocum's lips.

Slocum drank, then nodded his thanks.

"Did Sam tell you much about the mayor?"

"Not a lot."

"He's a pretty bad character. Or at least he lets himself be used by some pretty bad characters. We want the ledgers so we can force him to step down.''

''That's why I want them. I want to show people that Sam was actually a hero.''

''Sam was a very decent man,'' the old woman said, ''when he let himself be.''

''This sounds like a frigging revival meeting,'' Gil said.

''Why don't you be quiet, Gil?''

The old woman leaned down, took a clean white cloth from her dress pocket, raised the glass and poured some of the water over the cloth, and then began to work on Slocum's bruised and battered face.

''They sure love their work, those two,'' the old woman said to Gil. ''That's why I don't want them around.''

''We need men like that if we're going up against the mayor,'' Gil said. ''We need men exactly like that.''

But the old woman was all business now, leaning in close to Slocum's face, using the damp cloth carefully.

''What happens to me now?'' Slocum said.

''Why, I thought you knew,'' the old woman said.

''Knew what?''

''I'm going to take you to a very special place.''

''Oh, yeah?''

''Yes. And we're going to meet a very special person.''

''Who?''

''Eve McKay.''

# 13

*My Dearest Eve,*

*All your life you've thought of me as your Aunt Belle. But now I must tell you the truth—a truth that will be painful for both of us to hear.*

*I am your mother.*

*In your very early life, I was run out of several cities. In one city, I was even tarred and feathered. No matter where I went, people seemed to know who I was. Snickered at me. Whispered about me. A few times I even tried to give up being a prostitute but one way or another, I was always dragged back into the life.*

*Finally, when you were two years old, I decided that if I was going to be a prostitute, then I was going to be a prostitute unlike any the world had ever seen before.*

*I found a teacher who educated me; a dressmaker who taught me the basic principles of fashion; and a lawyer who introduced me to the precepts of law.*

*I went to Cleveland, found the prettiest girls available, and put them all through a scaled-down version of my own education.*

*Soon, the upper crust of the city was no longer interested in uncouth street girls. They wanted the kind of girl they could find only in the mansion I had bought and redecorated.*

*I duplicated this success in several cities. By this time, you were old enough to ask questions.*

*It was time to tell you the truth—but I couldn't. Not quite.*

*I knew you would be ashamed if you thought that your mother was a prostitute, so I invented the story that your mother had been a nurse who died while helping others during a cholera outbreak. I told you that you were then given to me to raise.*

*But now it's time you know the truth.*

*You're twenty years old and you are already pulling away from me. I know that you value your part in the reform movement that will oust the mayor.*

*I just don't want to see you get hurt. You took the ledgers from my den—where the mayor had left them to go out with me—and turned them over to Sam Myles. I know you see him as a hero, but to me he was pretty typical of the charming drifter-type I've met all my life. Believe me, my darling, eventually he would have let you down. He would have kept the ledgers for himself and blackmailed the mayor with them.*

*But enough about what divides us.*

*I would like you to come here at 6:00 tonight. I want to spend some time with you—as my daughter, not my "niece."*

*I realize that you may well never forgive me for my deception—but I pray you do.*

*I kept the truth from you to spare your feelings and for no other reason.*

*Sincerely Yours,*
*Your Mother*

# 14

The old woman led Slocum upstairs to the second floor, where he was put, at gunpoint, in a small dusty room, strapped to a straight-back chair, and hit twice by Gil the bartender before the old woman could stop him.

When Gil went to slap Slocum the third time, the old woman put herself between them and took the blow herself.

"That's just like you, Gil, slapping a woman," the old lady said.

Gil scowled and left the room.

She went over and closed the door behind him, then turned back to Slocum.

"You'll meet Eve very soon."

"You sound like you're going somewhere."

"I am. We're supposed to have a meeting in the basement."

"With who?"

"The merchants the mayor's people extort money from. He takes twenty percent of everything."

"Twenty percent? That much?"

She shook her gray head. "He's weak, but he has

very strong people around him. Strong and cruel. Some of the things he's done to the merchants and their families . . .''

"There's a cop named Halliwell who says he's on your side."

"I wouldn't trust a San Francisco cop under any circumstances."

"You may be wrong about Halliwell."

"I doubt it."

"So when will you be back?"

"An hour at most."

"And you'll bring Eve with you?"

"Yes. But she'll ask you the same question we did."

"What question?"

"What does 'Silver Stallion' mean?"

"I don't have any idea."

"That's what Sam Myles told her the day before he was killed. She asked him where the ledgers were and he said, 'They're safe. The Silver Stallion is watching over them.' So he didn't say anything to you like that?"

"Not a word."

She smiled. "I'm an old lady. It would be most discourteous to lie to me."

He shrugged. "I guess you'll just have to take my word for it, ma'am. I never heard of any Silver Stallion till I came here." He paused and watched her face carefully. "You seem like a pretty decent lady."

"Why, thank you."

"I just hope you're not going to turn on me when I get my hands on Gil."

She laughed. "No, Mr. Slocum, I don't rightly think I will. In fact, if I were a man, I would've kicked Gil's butt a long time ago." She consulted the small railroad watch she had pinned to the front of her dowdy gray dress. "Time for the merchants to meet. I'll be back as soon as I can. Then we'll get this all straightened out."

"Meaning you'll let me go?"

She smiled. "Yes, Mr. Slocum, meaning I'll let you go."

# 15

At the announcement of the name, Henry Carvelle looked up from his desk, startled.

"Who did you say?"

"A Mr. Asbury, sir," his matronly secretary announced. Miss Pym of the pince-nez; Miss Pym of the rustling bustle.

"Kenneth Asbury?"

"Yessir."

"Waiting to see me?"

"Yessir."

"My God."

Why would Kenneth Asbury, the man who ran most of the underworld activity in San Francisco, come himself to the mayor's office? There was a silent agreement that Asbury would never be implicated in any criminal activities. Leave that to underlings. As far as the community at large knew, Asbury was old-line money who spent his days helping raise funds for art galleries and symphonies.

What the hell was going on?

"Send him in."

"Yessir."

"And don't interrupt us."

"Yessir."

"And don't tell anybody you saw him here."

"No sir." Beat. "Sir?"

"Yes?"

"Are you all right?"

"Of course I'm all right. Why wouldn't I be all right?"

"It's just that you seem so . . ."

"I seem so what?"

"Agitated is the word, I guess, sir."

"I'm not agitated at all. Now get the hell out of here and bring Asbury in."

"Yessir."

"Agitated," the mayor of San Francisco snorted. "Agitated."

The man who entered the mayor's office a few moments later was a man in his late forties who had put on some unwanted weight lately but who carried the extra pounds with a kind of brute force. For all his poise and intelligence, there was something primitive and angry about Kenneth Asbury. Not even the Edwardian cut of his suit, not even the diamond stickpin in his cravat, not even the pomade on his gray-shot black hair could quite civilize him completely.

He put out a hand that the mayor was afraid to take.

Kenneth Asbury's handshake was famous. He could have brought even a circus strongman to his knees with that grip.

He was that powerful. And he knew it. And he delighted in it.

The mayor decided not to be humiliated. Just as his

secretary was closing the door, Henry Carvelle waved Asbury into a leather chair.

"You don't look well, Henry," Asbury said as he sat down.

Oh, great, the mayor thought. First Miss Pym with her "agitated" nonsense, and now Asbury with his "You don't look well, Henry."

"I've never felt better, Kenneth."

"You look a little nervous too," Asbury said. Then he looked around the office. "You really should let one of my decorators do this place over for you."

"I like it fine."

"The mayor deserves better than imitation Ming dynasty vases and some very queer wall coverings."

"I don't find them 'queer' at all."

"Not even a little bit effeminate?"

Carvelle groaned. This was typical treatment from Asbury, a man who loved to undermine him.

"Not the least bit effeminate, Mr. Asbury." He leaned forward, steepling his fingers. "I'm not sure it was wise coming here."

"Believe me, I thought it over for a long time."

"Then why—"

"Because, Henry, you don't seem to be getting the fucking point."

Even though Asbury had spoken softly, his words lashed the air like a whip.

"I see."

"No, you don't see, Henry. You don't see at all."

Now it was Asbury who was agitated. He sat straight up in his chair. Even though he was several feet from the mayor, Carvelle felt as if Asbury was right in his face.

"You mean the ledgers?"

"Of course I mean the ledgers, Henry," Asbury said. "What the fuck else would I mean?"

"It's under control."

"Since when?"

Henry allowed himself a tiny smug smile. "Since I devised a way to get Eve McKay back here with those books."

"And just how the hell do you propose to do that?"

So Henry Carvelle told him.

The plan, spoken aloud this way, sounded even better than it had earlier—sleek, efficient, clever—just the way, in fact, that the mayor thought of himself.

"It doesn't make any sense," Asbury said.

"What doesn't?"

"Your plan doesn't."

"My plan doesn't make any sense?"

"Are you hard of hearing, Henry? No, your plan doesn't make any sense."

Here the mayor had been expecting applause, but all he got was—

"Even if she comes back to visit her mother, there's no guarantee she'll bring the books along."

"But her own mother?" the mayor said. "She'll want to bring the ledgers along so she can get her mother out of trouble with you and me."

Asbury stood and began to pace.

"So this is your idea of a plan? God, Henry, you really are a stupid fucking man, you know that? When I put you in this office, I thought you'd at least be careful about things." He shook his head. "I never dreamed you'd be stupid enough to take our ledgers over to your whore's living quarters."

"She isn't a whore."

"Oh, no, then what is she, Henry? A nun maybe? Is she a nun?"

"Well, whatever she is, she isn't a whore. Not anymore anyway."

Asbury laughed. "Did she have her hymen sewed back in, Henry?"

"I won't tell jokes about the woman I love."

Asbury stood at the window, looking down at fashionable San Francisco, shaking his head. "This all started going badly when you had that old reporter killed, Henry. Kessler, I mean."

"He was on to us."

"He wasn't on to jack shit."

"He knew that I was part of the underworld."

"God, Henry, everybody in the city knows that. Proving it is all that matters. And nobody can prove it. Nobody at all."

"Kessler could have," said the mayor, "if I'd let him keep investigating me."

"So you had him murdered and now every day the newspapers are making more insinuations about the corrupt mayor."

"I didn't have any choice but to have him killed."

"You had plenty of choices, Henry."

The mayor opened his mouth to defend himself again, but gave up—mostly because he agreed with Asbury. Ever since Kessler had been murdered, everything had started going wrong, ending with Eve McKay stealing the ledgers.

Now everything was very much in jeopardy.

Asbury walked over to another window for another view of the street below. "Do we know for sure that this Eve McKay even has the ledgers anymore?" he said after a time.

"Sure we do."

"What makes you so sure?"

"She took them, didn't she?" the mayor said.

"Just because she took them doesn't mean she still has them, Henry." Asbury had gone back to speaking to a very slow child.

"She has them. I'm sure of it. And she's going to bring them over tonight. I'm sure of that too. And then I'll take the ledgers from her."

Asbury faced him fully now. "If I don't have those ledgers by midnight, Henry, I'm going to personally take care of you myself."

"Personally take care of me? Is that a threat?"

Asbury smiled. "Good old Henry. So quick on the uptake. Of course it's a fucking threat, you stupid asshole. Of course it's a threat."

Asbury moved to the door. "Another thing."

"Yes?"

"Your Miss Pym?"

"What about her?"

"For God's sake, why don't you get somebody presentable to the public? You're the one who knows all the whores, Henry. Certainly you could do better than Miss Pym."

"She's just what this office needs."

"Oh? Humorless and dried up and cranky? Is that what this office needs, Henry?"

"She's very efficient."

"I'll bet."

"And very—pleasant—when she wants to be."

"Let me know when that is, Henry—when she's pleasant, I mean. I'd love to come in and see that for myself, Miss Pym being pleasant. We might have the eighth wonder of the world here."

Asbury's sarcasm was wearing.

The mayor felt worn out now, in need of a nap and maybe—unmanly as it might be—a cry. He felt sad and scared and very isolated. He wanted to flee into the arms of Belle Kelly—the same woman Asbury had just called a whore—but because it was her daughter who had taken the ledgers . . . Well, Henry had never felt more alone.

Nobody to turn to.

Nowhere to run.

"Everything will be fine," said the mayor to the real boss of San Francisco.

Asbury opened the door, and looked back at Henry with the full brute force of his gaze. "Things had better be all right, Henry. They had damned well better be all right."

# 16

Slocum couldn't be sure, but it seemed to him that the old woman who had promised to come back and free him was seriously late. Gone much longer than the hour she'd promised.

Where the hell was she? Had she decided to go back on her word?

One thing he had to say for Gil the bartender, the sonofabitch sure knew how to tie knots. Slocum couldn't move either his wrists or his ankles more than an eighth of an inch in any direction. Of course, moving at all wasn't much fun, not after the beating he'd taken.

He started daydreaming again about taking his vengeance on Gil.

Oh, yes, Slocum was going to have himself one hell of a time.

One hell of a time.

Across town, in the hotel that Slocum had selected, young Lilly was using her peashooter on the thug she'd hogtied after he'd tried to break in.

Lilly always carried sharp-edged tiny pebbles in her

pockets so she could use her peashooter when she needed to.

Most grown-ups looked at her shooter as a toy. But then why should she expect grown-ups to know anything more about peashooters than they knew about anything else?

She hit the thug right in the forehead.

He worried against the ropes on his wrists and ankles. "You little bitch. You just wait till I get free."

"Yeah? And when's that going to be, Muldoon? Two years from now?"

"It's goin' your way right now, but you wait'n' see. I'll have the upper hand real soon."

"Oooh, you're really scary."

And with that, she hit him in the forehead.

"Damn you."

"Well, damn you too, Muldoon. Now, tell me what you were looking for in this room."

"I ain't tellin' you shit."

This time she got him on the nose. She giggled. "You really looked funny there, Muldoon. When I hit you, your eyes crossed."

"Little bitch."

"Big asshole."

"Rotten pig."

She grinned. "That's what I like about you, Muldoon. You're so mature."

She launched another pea at him. This one hit him in the forehead again.

"You know, maybe I should paint a target right on your forehead. Yeah, that could be fun."

"Bitch," Muldoon said.

• • •

"His name's Chan."

Halliwell stood in the sunny open door of the kitchen.

His wife, Miriam, turned from the sink, wiped her hands on her frilly apron, and said, "Chan?"

Chan nodded, and put out his hand.

She took it, shook it, and smiled. Then she looked up at her husband for some clue as to why he'd brought this boy home.

"With Bobby's birthday coming up and all . . ." Halliwell paused. "Well, I just thought it might make things a little easier for you if you had Chan here."

"I see."

"He seems like he's a real nice boy."

Chan nodded. "I don't like to brag, Mrs. Halliwell, but I am a really nice boy."

"And he seems honest and bright and friendly," Halliwell said.

"Those are the three things I work really hard at, Mrs. Halliwell, being honest and bright and friendly."

She smiled. "And what else do you work hard at?"

"Oh, just trying to be as irresistible as possible, I guess."

"Lord save us," Miriam Halliwell said, "he's as touched with the blarney as your Irish in-laws." She leaned over and held her arms out. Chan, with no urging at all, ran to her and gave her a hug.

As she was holding on to Chan, she looked up at her husband, who was quick to notice the tears in her eyes.

"Thanks," she whispered to him. "Thanks."


As the meeting with the merchants was breaking up in Fat Amy's, the old lady started up the stairs to where Slocum was tied up.

She was running much later than she'd predicted.

Slocum was probably pretty angry.

She had just started up the stairs when one of the greasy men who worked in the bar said, "Letter for Eve McKay. Can you get it to her?"

The old lady nodded, took the envelope, and started up the stairs.

There was a name written on the Return Address lines: Belle Kelly.

But why would Belle Kelly be writing her a letter?

# 17

Before she got a chance to read the letter, Gil came up to the old woman and said, "I'm going up to take care of Slocum."

She grabbed his wrist. "You're angry with him because he embarrassed you in the bar. You know he's on our side. There's no reason to hurt him at all. I want to let him go."

Gil's hand lashed out, slamming the old lady against the wall. "Your friend Sam Myles is barely in the ground and you're already flirting with a new one."

Her slap came up and cracked against Gil's face. "You have no right to say that. You know how much I loved Sam. I just don't want to see Slocum hurt. And I won't let him be hurt, you understand that?"

The old lady's body shook with rage, intimidating Gil.

"Do you understand what I'm saying, Gil?"

He muttered something.

"Do you, Gil?"

"Yes, I understand."

"I'm going to untie him and let him go."

"He's working for the mayor. You'll see. You think

you're clever—just like the rest of the merchants think they're clever—but you're not. You'll be sorry you didn't let me kill him now.''

And with that, he stalked into the bar.

In three minutes, Gil had had two drinks of whiskey. He was just pouring himself another one when one of the whores came up to him.

''Copper hassled me again this morning,'' she said. ''You told me to tell ya when it happened again.''

''Thanks, Betty.''

''Hassled me for money—and got about two dozen cheap feels. I wish I had the crabs just so I could give 'em to the coppers.''

''Won't be long now, Betty.''

''What won't be long now?''

''Before we get 'em off our back.''

''You really think so, Gil?''

As he stood there, angry and bitter, he thought to himself: If I'd been running this fucking show, we would have turned those ledgers over to the newspapers by now and brought down the mayor. But they don't listen to me because I don't own this place. Owners only listen to each other. . . .

''I'm gonna take care of things, Betty. You'll see.''

She leaned over and kissed him on the cheek. ''You're a nice guy, Gil. A real nice guy.''

She left him alone to his drinking.

The old woman sat on the second-floor stairs reading the letter in total disbelief.

Belle Kelly was actually Eve McKay's mother and not her aunt?

But how could that possibly be? All these years, she'd thought . . .

Slocum looked up as the door opened. The old woman came quietly into the room, closing the door behind her. Her face, eyes, and cheeks sparkled with tears. A letter dangled from her fingers.

She took one step toward him and said, "I'm going to let you go, Mr. Slocum."

He looked at her tear-streaked face. "What happened?"

"Nothing that would interest you, Mr. Slocum. It's just a personal matter."

"You didn't happen to find Eve McKay for me, did you?" he said.

"Yes, I did as a matter of fact."

And with that, the old lady reached up to her scalp, took hard hold of her hair, and jerked it backwards.

She then unbuttoned the ugly gray dress she was wearing.

With the gray wig gone, she showed herself to be a fetching redhead.

With her gray dress gone, she showed herself to be a young and attractive woman in a simple blue frock that amply displayed her charms.

Even with her heavy makeup on, she was a very pretty girl.

"I'm Eve McKay, Mr. Slocum. I started wearing this disguise yesterday, after Sam was killed. I knew the mayor's men would think I had the ledgers."

"And you don't know where they are?"

"No. I wish I did."

"Do you have any idea what 'Silver Stallion' means?"

"No. None of us do. Sam just told me that the ledgers were safe. That nobody could get past the Silver Stallion. He didn't want to tell me what it meant because he said it was too dangerous to know—that if they got him, they'd come after me." She smiled sadly. "They've come after me anyway."

Slocum shook his head. "We'd better find out what it means before the mayor does."

"I know. He has so many men out combing the city that he's bound to turn up something pretty soon." She paused a moment. "All I can think of is Father Michaels."

"Who's that?"

"A good friend of his. You might not believe it, but Sam was a good Catholic. Never missed Mass on Sunday. Went to confession every Saturday."

"Trying to reform himself?"

"Right. He really did want to change his ways."

"He might have told this priest?"

"Possibly. He's worth seeing anyway."

"Where's his parish?"

"St. Angela's. Not too far from Sam's office."

"You going to cut me loose?"

"Yes."

"Good. Then the first thing I'll do is go visit this Father Michaels. You want to go along?"

The misty look came back to her eyes. "No. There's somebody else I need to go see."

"You sure it isn't anything I can help you with?"

"I wish you could, John. But it really is very personal."

She came over and started to untie his wrists, but before she got very far the door slammed open.

Gil stood in the doorway with a .45 in one hand and

a hunting knife in another. The blade was streaked with dried blood. Very theatrical but effective.

"Get out of here, Eve."

"No. I want to untie him."

"I'm taking this over, Eve. And now we'll get some things done."

She started to lunge toward him, but Slocum called out to her. No sense in her getting hurt too.

"Go on out, Eve. I'll be fine."

"Are you sure?"

Slocum nodded.

Gil paid no attention to her now. She might as well not have been here. His entire being was focused on Slocum, the man who had humiliated him downstairs in front of the customers. A bartender had a certain decorum, a certain dignity that had to be maintained. You didn't go throwing him around asshole-over-appetite in front of his regular clients. Or if you did—you paid for it.

"Go on," Slocum said to Eve. "I'll be fine."

She raised the letter up and glanced at it again. Whatever news she'd gotten must have been sorrowful indeed to make her look and act this way.

"Go on," Slocum said. "Please."

She looked at Gil, looked at Slocum, nodded, and left.

"Close the door," Gil said.

She quietly closed the door behind her.

Gil walked over to Slocum and hit him on the side of the face with the barrel of the .45.

"I hope you like pain, cowboy, 'cause you're sure gonna get a lot of it."

He struck him again.

"That one feel any better?"

"Felt great."

"You talk tough, cowboy. At least for now."

He hit him again.

And that was when Slocum played his little surprise on him.

Eve had loosened the rope around his wrists just enough so that he could start to work his hands free. It had taken a few minutes to get them completely free, but now he had his old friends, his iron fists, back again.

He delivered an uppercut that startled Gil and pushed him clear across the room into the wall.

As Gil grappled to regain his composure, Slocum quickly started to untie his ankles.

He was about halfway finished when Gil vaulted off the wall and came running at him with the hunting knife.

Apparently Gil wanted the satisfaction of making his kill personal. With a knife instead of the more impersonal pistol.

He jumped on Slocum, trying to bury the knife deep in Slocum's shoulder.

The door was flung open.

Eve McKay stood there with a shotgun.

"All right, Gil. Let him alone."

Slocum said, still grappling with Gil, "We both want this, Eve. We really do."

Gil grunted his agreement.

The knife slashed across Slocum's shoulder, tearing fabric and flesh alike.

Eve screamed when she saw the blood.

But she knew that Slocum was serious about both of them wanting this duel. It was a blood feud now—inevitable as it was deadly.

Blood streaming down his shoulder, Slocum managed to connect with another uppercut, freeing him from the chair.

He climbed out of his ankle ropes and then started circling Gil.

The man seemed to be a skilled knife fighter, throwing the blade from one hand to another while always constantly circling.

If Slocum wasn't careful here, he was going to get his white cowboy ass sliced into about twenty thousand pieces.

He lunged.

But it was exactly what Gil had wanted him to do because just as Slocum lunged close, Gil was able to lean in and slash a deep gash across Slocum's chest.

Yes, indeed, Gil here knew just what he was doing.

Slocum had to be mighty careful.

They started circling each other again.

When he reached the ankle ropes that lay on the floor, Slocum reached down and grabbed them.

The rope stretched to maybe three feet. As he continued to circle, Slocum wrapped half the rope around his knuckles. The other half was free.

Gil tried very hard to smirk off whatever Slocum had in mind, but it didn't work. He watched fascinated as Slocum raised the rope and started to whip it across.

It hit Gil right in the eye.

The thing didn't hurt but it stung, and worse—it momentarily blinded him in that eye.

Gil could feel himself rock forward, losing his balance.

"You fucker," Gil said.

"Better watch your mouth in front of a lady," Slocum said.

They went back to circling.

Gil's entire body shook with anger. He wanted to find

Slocum's heart and plunge the knife in deep, again and again.

Slocum lunged again.

And Gil was waiting for him again.

This time he opened up a wound on Slocum's opposite shoulder. The streaming blood was considerable.

A few more circles.

Slocum raised his rope again.

He started to play with Gil, enjoying himself.

Slocum would look as if he were about to lash out at Gil—then stop.

But not before Gil's attention would be totally diverted by the rope and Gil would once more lose his balance.

"You fucker," Gil said again.

Slocum did this three times in a row and Gil, who was black of heart but also empty of head, went for it each time. Each time he started to lose balance, cursed Slocum, and got so mad that his forgot to keep his knife hand straight and ready.

The fourth time Slocum raised his rope, he really did lash out, hitting Gil in the eye again—same eye, same place, same result. Gil teared up, blinked, and lost sight in that eye.

And now Slocum lunged again.

And as he lunged, he brought up his right foot and let it arc directly into Gil's crotch.

Gil cried out.

Slocum now kicked him in the ribs, hearing bones break as he did so.

But somehow Gil still held on to his blade.

"Put the knife down," Slocum said. "We'll finish this with fists."

"Fuck yourself, cowboy," Gil said.

Once again, they started to circle.

Slowly, slowly, they moved around the room, each waiting for his best chance, each eager to kill the other man.

There would be no second chances and both men knew it.

They'd each have one opportunity to kill the other man—and if that failed . . .

Gil lunged first, a surprisingly skillful lunge that let him cut a gash in the side of Slocum's neck.

This time it was Slocum who cried out.

But even as he was temporarily overwhelmed by pain, Slocum grabbed the knife wrist of the other man and started to wrestle him to the floor.

By the time they reached the floor, Gil had fallen on his own knife, and blood was bubbling in his mouth.

"Oh, God," Eve McKay said, "look at him."

Death was setting in quickly and quietly. Gil had made no noise.

Slocum rolled him over on his back. Gil's eyes were already glazed. The knife had entered directly into his heart.

"I'm sorry, Gil," Slocum said.

Gil looked up and smiled with bad teeth. "Go fuck yourself, cowboy."

And died.

Twenty minutes later, in her own room, Eve finished cleaning Slocum's wounds. None were serious, but they sure were messy. She even managed to find him a shirt that fit.

She glanced at the letter on the bureau. "I really need to go now, John. I'll see you back here tonight."

"You sure you don't want me along?"

"No," she said, kissing him tenderly on the cheek, "but you're sweet to offer."

She stood up, walked over to her bureau, took out a fifth of good whiskey, and handed it to him. "Brand-new. I've been saving it for a special occasion. So far I haven't found one."

"Appreciate it."

He yawned.

"You need some rest, John, whether you think so or not."

"You may be right."

"Why don't you let me fix you up on that couch over there?"

"You've done a hell of a lot for me already."

"C'mon, now, let me play mom for a minute."

So she got him all tucked into bed, and he had to admit that he could barely keep his eyes open.

This time she kissed him on the forehead. Then she left.

He woke up an hour later, poured himself a drink of the good whiskey, and while he was sipping, happened to notice that she'd left her letter behind.

He hobbled over to the bureau, picked it up, read it, and said, "God, Eve, you're walking right into their trap."

Slocum grabbed his hat, gun, and another quick snort of whiskey, and then got the hell out of there.

# 18

The man, an otherwise sober and respectable man, sat in a prim straight-back chair telling Belle Kelly what it was he wanted. And what he wanted was anything but sober and respectable.

He was unable to look at her as he spoke.

"Two of them."

"Two. Fine," she said, as if he were ordering apples or tomatoes.

"And no older than eleven."

"All right."

"Twins, if possible. I've always had this—well, I've always thought about twins."

She smiled without humor. "You don't make this easy."

"It's my fiftieth birthday. I want to make it memorable."

"All right."

"And if they could be wearing First Communion dresses."

"Certainly."

"Very lacy and—virginal."

"Of course."

"That would be the first part of the evening."

"The young twins?"

"Yes."

"And the second part of the evening?" Belle inquired.

"A Negro."

"A Negro."

"A big, fat Negro with huge breasts."

"All right. Any particular age?"

"Thirties, early forties."

"Any special costume?"

"Stark naked."

She wrote all this down. "Stark naked," she repeated.

"And with a good voice."

"A good voice?"

"Singing voice. When we're done and I'm all tired out, I want her to sing to me."

"Ah."

"Stephen Foster."

"Stephen Foster. Of course."

"I love Stephen Foster's songs, don't you?"

"Oh, yes," Belle said, "I hum them all the time."

This man was much stranger than she'd ever imagined—so strange that he had ceased to amuse her.

Now he was just one more very strange man who vaguely frightened her.

He was the kind of man who went crazy in whorehouses, moving through them with a machete, lopping off heads and breasts and arms and legs as he spouted Bible passages and told the Lord that he was slaughtering these people in His honor.

A discreet knock.

"Excuse me," Belle said, and went to the door.

Cyrus, the old Negro who had been with her the past twenty years, whispered, "She's here, Miss Belle."

"Eve?"

"Yes'm."

"Good. Have her wait in the drawing room. I'll be in momentarily."

"Fine. And Miss Belle?"

"Yes."

"There's something you should know."

"Yes?"

"The mayor, he put a couple of men outside our doors."

She started to say, "But he promised . . ." Then she stopped herself.

Better never to show indecision or fear to employees. Better always to appear in command.

"They're armed, these men?"

"Yes'm."

"And they're at the front door?"

"Yes'm. And the back."

"Thank you, Cyrus."

"Yes'm," said the old man with the white woolly hair. He shot her something resembling a bow and then disappeared.

She stood leaning against the door a moment.

Henry Carvelle had promised her that Eve would not be held or injured in any way. If she had the ledgers, fine. But if she didn't have the ledgers, then Henry would believe her and let her go.

But now Belle wondered.

Henry was such a weak bastard. If his cronies demanded that he hurt Belle . . .

She should never have agreed to lure Eve up here.

She loved Eve so much—

"I'm in kind of a hurry, Belle," said the man behind her. "Tonight there's a church social I'm supposed to go to with my family."

Ah, of course, Belle thought. Never forget about the hypocrisy of her clients.

Go up to the whorehouse and roll around with two eleven-year-olds and a voluptuous black nanny, and then go home and wash off the pussy smells and get yourself ready to go play the good Methodist family man for the evening.

Belle went back and sat down. "Now, is there anything else you want me to write down on your list?"

The otherwise sober and respectable man looked even more embarrassed than before. Once again, his eyes fell. He could not look at Belle. "Well, there's one thing, I guess."

"Yes."

"I've never tried an amputee."

"An amputee?"

"You know. Somebody with a missing limb or two."

"Ah. An amputee."

"I suppose that sounds kind of twisted."

"Not at all. Lots of people ask for amputees."

He looked up, surprised. "They do?"

"All the time."

What a sick fuck he was, Belle thought. Little girls, Negro mammies, and now amputees.

Somebody should do him the favor of shooting him on the spot.

Right on the frigging spot.

"God, that makes me feel better, Belle. Knowing that a lot of people ask for amputees."

"All the time," Belle said. "All the time."

# 19

As Slocum left Fat Amy's, he glanced across the street and saw his pal, the man with the bowler, striped suit, and walking stick, standing in the shade of an overhang, watching Fat Amy's door.

Slocum still wondered who the hell the guy was and what he wanted.

Unfortunately, he'd already shown that he wasn't going to be caught easily, and there just wasn't time now to try anything fancy.

Slocum hurried on his way to the hotel. He wanted to see how the girl Lilly was doing. He also wanted to see if she could tell him where he'd find Belle Kelly.

Halliwell didn't usually come home so early in the evening, but today was different.

Today he wanted to see how his wife was getting along with Chan, the street kid he'd brought home.

He came through the back gate, a detective who looked like a detective with his strong purposeful face and strong purposeful stride, and paused there as he heard laughter coming from the screened door in back.

Chan first; then Miriam, Halliwell's wife.

Laughter. Not a familiar sound since the terrible day their own boy had been stricken ill with fever and died.

Halliwell went up to the back door and put his ear to the screen.

"You're really good at checkers, Chan," Miriam was saying from the front room.

"I play a lot."

"You must. You've beaten me every game."

"I still think you're letting me win sometimes."

Miriam giggled like a girl. "You shouldn't say that, Chan. You know it's not true."

But just from the sound of her amusement, Halliwell could tell that it was true indeed.

"Are you hungry, Chan?"

Now it was his turn to giggle. "Let's see, I've already had two cookies."

"And a small bowl of popcorn."

"And a small dish of ice cream."

"And a piece of chocolate."

"And a glass of milk."

"And a glass of soda," Miriam said.

"Yes," Chan said. "I'm starving!"

Miriam was laughing as she came out to the kitchen, calling over her shoulder, "I've got one piece of pound cake left and it's all yours."

Then she looked over and saw her husband in the doorway.

"Hello."

"Hello," he said.

"You look so happy standing there. You're grinning like a little kid."

"I take it you two are getting along."

For months, she'd resisted his every effort to adopt a

child. She was too old to risk childbirth and adoption was the only other option.

"You must like it out there."

"Huh?"

"Outdoors."

"Oh."

"Otherwise you'd come inside and give your wife a kiss."

"That sounds like a good idea."

He opened the door, walked in, and took her in his arms.

"And you'd also tell your wife why you're home so early."

"I just wanted to see how things were going."

"They're going fine."

"So I see."

He kissed her. If you had to measure it out, the kiss was comprised of one-fourth platonic love, two-fourths romantic love, and one-fourth plain and simple human respect. There was no human being on this earth whom he admired or loved more.

"He's a wonderful boy," she said.

"Indeed he is," Halliwell said, "and I saw that right away."

"Do we just—keep him?"

"I think so. Just—make him ours."

"He's so smart. Just like . . ." She stopped herself. Tears shone in her eyes. "I feel guilty. I have to say it, darling. I know it's not the right thing to say—but I feel guilty because now he's going to take the place of Bobby."

"I know."

"I don't want it to seem that I'm pushing Bobby from my memory or anything."

"I know you're not, dear."

"So it's all right if I enjoy my time with Chan? I'm not betraying Bobby?"

"It's fine, dear," he said, holding her tighter. "It's fine."

He held her for a long moment, then let her go. "I have to go upstairs a moment."

"Oh. Now I understand."

"Understand what?"

"Why you came home."

"To see how you and Chan were doing."

"Yes, and I believe you when you say that—but there's something else too, isn't there?"

"Well . . ."

"Your Navy Colt."

"Well . . ."

"You must be getting nearer to finding those ledgers."

He laughed and kissed her on the cheek. "There's nothing like being married to a woman who can read minds."

"So you are getting closer to finding the ledgers?"

Halliwell nodded solemnly. He was once again all cop. "I met a man named John Slocum. One way or another, I think he's going to lead me to the ledgers."

"Is he a good man or a bad man, this Slocum?"

"A little of both, I think. I doubt if even he could answer that question."

"So now you're going to get your father's gun?"

"Exactly," Halliwell said.

He usually carried the standard Smith & Wesson that the police department issued him years ago. But when there was a very difficult assignment about to conclude, he always came home and got his father's Navy Colt. His father had been a San Francisco cop—and an honest one—for twelve years before he was shot to death while chasing a robbery suspect.

Halliwell gave his wife another quick kiss and then went upstairs and got his father's gun.

# 20

Slocum did the knock. The code knock that would tell Lilly on the other side of the door who was here.

No answer.

Slocum stood in the hallway of the hotel trying to look natural as a fat middle-aged couple hustled past with their carpetbags.

He would probably look like that someday, he thought. Then: Holy shit, I hope not.

When the middle-aged couple disappeared around the corner of the hall, Slocum went back to tapping out the code.

Where the hell was Lilly? Why hadn't she answered the first time? All sorts of terrible images came to his mind. There was no answer this time either. And she had the only key. Time for Slocum to do a little lock-picking. He set to work.

As soon as the lock was open, he took out his gun.

He went in fast, ducking and swerving so he wouldn't be an easy target. But he didn't have to worry. The only person in this room capable of firing a weapon was presently tied up—as in lashed, hand and foot, to a chair.

"What the hell happened to you, Lilly?" Slocum said.

Then he realized that no matter how many questions he asked, he wasn't going to get any answer. In addition to being all trussed up, Lilly had also been gagged.

He got the gag off.

"That asshole," she said.

"Which asshole?"

"The one who tried to break in here."

"Looks like he did a good job of it."

"Like hell he did. I tied him up."

"I see."

"You're smirking, aren't you?"

"No, I'm not. Honest."

"You're smirking, you asshole. You think just because I'm a girl, I don't know how to tie people up. Well, for your information, I had that asshole tied so tight he could barely move."

"So what happened?"

"He rubbed the ropes against the bedpost until they got loose."

The better part of valor was not asking how, if she'd been watching him, he'd managed to do that. He didn't really want to know anyway. "Did you find out who he was working for?"

"Of course. I pistol-whipped the hell out of him."

"Good girl."

"He was working for the mayor, who else?"

"Looking for the ledgers your father mentioned?"

She nodded. "Looking for the ledgers."

"You up for a little excitement?"

"Like what?"

"Like getting a princess down from a tower."

"Huh?"

"As soon as you tell me where Belle Kelly keeps

house, we'll go over there and start working on that princess.''

"You're a crazy bastard, Slocum, you know that?''

"And you've got a dirty mouth for a sweet little girl.''

"A sweet little girl?'' Lilly said. "Shit, I wasn't a sweet little girl when I was three.''

Slocum grinned. "You know, somehow I believe that.''

# 21

Just before entering the drawing room, Belle took in a sharp breath, then silently muttered a sort of prayer. Hookers weren't worthy enough to say a real prayer, she reasoned. She could only say a silent prayer.

Sunlight gave the drawing room a soft, sunny glow. Most of the furnishings were of white fabric and thus picked up the golden cast of the sun's rays.

Between two windows, on a small chaste divan, sat Eve, nervously playing with her fingers in her lap. She looked young and pretty and sad.

When Belle came in, Eve looked up. She too took in a sharp breath.

Belle came straight over to her and kissed her on the cheek.

Eve seemed to tolerate rather than enjoy it. She did not offer to touch her mother in return.

Belle went over, sat gracefully down in one of the big armchairs, and said, "So you've read my letter."

"Yes, I have."

"You seem angry."

"That's not the right word."

"Then what is the right word, Eve?"

Eve sighed. "I'm not sure."

"I thought I explained myself pretty well."

Eve looked at her mother for a time. "What you did was justify your deceit."

"I didn't deceive you, Eve."

"Of course you did."

"I kept the truth from you for your own good."

"No," Eve said, "you kept the truth from me for *your* own good. You didn't want me to know about you because you would have been ashamed."

"I've done what I had to to survive, Eve. And I've managed to keep us both alive."

Eve touched a hand to her forehead.

"Headache?"

"Yes," Eve said.

"Would you like me to get you something for it?"

"No, thank you."

They fell into silence again.

"After a while, I think you'll understand, and forgive me."

"I hope so, Mother."

"You know I love you."

"I know. And I love you. It's just . . ."

Belle waved a delicate hand. For such a successful woman in a man's world, she had managed to keep herself completely feminine. "Maybe I should have told you all along."

Gently, Eve said, "I'm just glad you told me."

"Did you ever suspect?"

"No." She smiled. "I guess I'm pretty naive in some ways."

Belle decided to quietly raise the subject she'd been avoiding. "I think you were naive about the ledgers too.

Especially about what Sam was going to do with them."

"I really believe in the reform movement, Mother." The smile again. "That seemed funny. Calling you Mother, I mean."

Belle smiled too. "Maybe you'll get used to it someday."

Eve glanced out the window. "I'm sure I sound very naive about this, but somebody has to start cleaning up San Francisco. Especially the mayor and the police department."

"It's a dangerous job."

"I know it's dangerous. That's why Sam Myles was the perfect man to do it. He'd been around so much. He wasn't afraid either."

Belle chose her words judiciously. "I'm not real sure Sam would have turned the ledgers over to reform politicians."

"But I am—sure, I mean."

"Sam's past . . ."

"But he'd changed, Mother. I know he'd changed because I'd seen him change."

Belle went over and poured herself some tea. Eve said she didn't want any.

Once she was seated again, Belle said, "Henry is of the mind that those ledgers are his and that he has the right to them. He wants you to hand them over today. Right now, in fact." As she sipped her tea, she looked at her daughter. A half-dozen feelings were reflected in her gaze: love, apprehension, pride, pleasure, sorrow, and even a little anger. She wished that Eve had been warmer about learning the truth. Belle had imagined this big emotional confrontation that ended with the two of them embracing and crying on each other's shoulder.

"I have to be honest here," Belle said.

"All right, Mother."

"Henry asked me to write you that letter."

"Henry? What's he got to do with it?"

"You've been hiding, dear. They managed to find Sam and you know what they did to him. But you've been hiding and they've been looking desperately for you. Henry couldn't think of any other way to get you up here, so . . ."

Eve sighed and went back to fidgeting with her fingers in her lap.

"I didn't want them to kill you, Eve. I thought if I got you up here, you'd see that it was best to turn the ledgers over and then everything would be all right."

"You may not believe this, Mother, but I don't have any idea where the ledgers are."

"You're serious?"

"Very serious."

"My God," Belle said. "I was sure you had them. I was sure we could get everything settled here today."

A knock.

Belle got up and hurried to the door.

Her old black friend.

"Yes?"

"The mayor, ma'am, he's waiting in the front room. He says he's goin' to come in."

"Tell him to wait."

"He says he won't wait, ma'am. I's sorry."

Belle knew how Henry got. No way this old black man was ever going to stop him from coming in here.

"Thank you," she said, and quietly closed the door.

"You have to be honest now, Eve. He'll be here in just a few seconds. You have to tell me where the ledgers are."

"But I don't know."

Belle flew to her, grabbed her by the slender shoulders, and shook her. "The truth, Eve. I need the truth."

"But that is the truth, Mother."

A knock.

This time she knew it would be Henry.

He would have one of his thugs with him.

He would—

"Eve, tell me where the ledgers are!"

But Henry had given up on knocking.

He flung the door back and came stalking in, a dandy with a large Colt in his right hand. He was followed by two men who looked as if they would take great pride in setting fire to orphans, nuns, and cripples.

"Hello, Eve," Henry said in his best imperious manner. "I've been listening to you and your mother. Your mother's right. It's time you be honest with her and tell her where you hid the ledgers."

"But I don't know where—" Eve started to say.

And Henry slapped her. Hard, right across the mouth, drawing blood.

"Henry—" Belle started to say.

Henry whirled on her and said, "I'm in charge here now, Belle. And let's remember that, all right?"

He nodded at Eve. "Tie her up."

# 22

The first thing they did, after they dragged Belle from the room and locked the door behind her, was rip away the top of Eve's dress so that her small but shapely breasts were exposed.

The second thing they did, after the one named Big Mike slapped Eve so hard she thought she would lose consciousness, was bind her with rope so coarse that it chewed into her flesh. This was done by the one named Rick.

"You gonna tell us where the ledgers are, little girl, or are we gonna have to get mean?" Mike said.

He obviously hoped they would have to get mean—though even now, even in these circumstances, Eve had to smile to herself.

Tearing away her dress and cutting into her flesh with rope—didn't that qualify as mean?

"What's so funny?" Mike said.

"You are."

"What the fuck's that supposed to mean?"

"Big and dumb," Eve said.

Rick snorted. "That's how I like 'em. Some real

spunk in 'em.'' He smiled at Big Mike. ''Gonna take us a while to break this little bitch down. And it's gonna be fun.''

''She's my daughter.''

''She's also the one person who can put all of us behind bars. You included, Belle.''

''She doesn't know where the ledgers are.''

''So she says.''

''She's not lying, Henry. She wouldn't lie to me.''

''Maybe you don't know her as well as you think.''

''No. I've only spent the last twenty years raising her.''

''People keep secrets.''

''Not Eve. She's always told me everything.''

''Yes; her good old trusting aunt. How did she take the news, by the way?''

''I think she's in a little bit of shock.''

''In other words, she didn't take it well.''

''She needs a little time is all.''

''She needs a little time, Belle—and I need those ledgers back.''

''If those men hurt her, I'll kill you.''

''She'll be fine.''

''She'd better be.''

''If she's sensible and tells them where the ledgers are, this will all be over very soon.''

''It had better be over soon, Henry. For your sake.''

Octavia Street was one of the most famous in all of San Francisco. The mansions there were envied throughout the world, even in the salons of Paris and the baronial estates of suburban London.

Slocum had never seen such estates before and, even

given the urgency of the moment, he took long enough to let himself be properly overwhelmed by the sweeping majesty of the huge Victorian homes displayed behind the cold iron fencing.

"Maybe you'll have a place like this someday," Lilly said. "If you start robbing banks."

"I'd have to rob a lot of banks to get a place like these. I'm not sure there are that many banks around."

They were walking quickly up a steep hill on top of which sat a foreboding Victorian mansion that seemed to loom above all the others as the shadows of dusk stretched long across the streets.

"That's a whorehouse?" Slocum said.

"Probably the nicest whorehouse you could find anywhere."

"So this is where Belle keeps her girls."

Lilly said, "I wish she'd hire me. I hear some of those girls make fifty dollars a night."

"I ever catch you turning into a whore, Lilly, I'll kick your ass from here to Sacramento."

"You ain't my pa."

"I may not be your pa, but I'd never stand by and watch you turn into a whore either."

She looked up at him and grinned. "What's the matter, Slocum, you don't think I'm pretty enough?"

"Oh, you're pretty enough. It's just that I want you to grow up to be a good family woman."

"Like you're a good family man?"

"Sarcastic little devil, aren't you?"

They had come to the gates.

The locked, iron gates.

"Well, Slocum," Lilly said, "you figured out how the hell we're going to get in there?"

• • •

Slocum spent the next fifteen minutes proving to both himself and Lilly that he had no idea how they were going to get past the iron gates.

"Gee, Slocum, and here I thought you were a regular hero. You know, like Nick Carter or somebody."

"Very funny."

He tried not to think of what was happening to Eve McKay.

"Shit," he said, shaking his head.

"You open to an idea from a snot-nosed kid who should keep her mouth shut if she knew her proper place?"

"Just what the hell are you talking about?"

She pointed to a Chinese couple slowly making their way toward the estate. They pushed a cart as they walked.

"Them?"

"Yes, Slocum, them. A lot of Chinese deliver fresh vegetables and fruits to these mansions."

"How's that gonna help us get inside?"

"Just calm down, Slocum, and leave everything to me. We'll be inside in five minutes."

Belle said, "I want to go in there."

"No."

"She's my daughter."

"They're not done with her yet."

"You sonofabitch."

"I didn't ask her to steal my ledgers."

"You bastard."

"Fix yourself a drink. This isn't like you, Belle. Going to pieces this way."

"No, it's more like you, isn't it, Mr. Mayor? Daddy's little boy."

"Don't get pissy, Belle. It's not becoming."

"I'll get a lot more than pissy. You wait and see."

Through the thick walls two rooms away, a scream could be heard. Eve's scream.

Belle rushed to the door.

The mayor grabbed her by the shoulders and spun her around. "It'll be over with soon, Belle. We'll have the ledgers and you'll have your daughter."

That was when Belle slapped him, as hard as a man would slap him.

"I'm going to kill you, Henry. I swear it."


"Wake her up."

"I'm tryin'. She ain't comin' around. I told you you hit her too hard."

"Bullshit. Take this rag and pour some water over it from that pitcher."

Half a minute later, Big Mike had the cold rag in his hand. He pressed it to Eve's forehead.

He couldn't keep his eyes off her tits. He wanted to suck on those little babies for a while. Big Mike had never had a girl half this fine before. It sure would be nice.

Her head was still slumped over.

"She's fakin' it," Big Mike said.

"I don't think so."

"You don't think so. Kiss my ass. I didn't hit her that hard."

"Maybe you didn't, but her head snapped back awful funny. And I seen her eyes go white."

Big Mike look down at her tits again. He'd like to see her pussy. He bet it'd be just as nice as her tits.

He knelt down next to her and took her hand. "We're done playin' games, darlin'," he said. "Now you sit up straight and open them eyes 'n talk to Big Mike. You understand me.''

''She ain't movin', Big Mike. She ain't movin' at all.''

Big Mike raised his hand, touched her cheek, and moved her head back. Her eyes were closed.

''You open them eyes, little lady. You hear me.''

But she said nothing.

''You hear me, little lady. You open them fuckin' eyes or Big Mike's gonna start slappin' you again.''

''Shit, man, you fuckin' killed her.''

And that was when she moaned. Not a big moan, not a dramatic moan, just a tiny little-girl moan, barely audible, but a moan nonetheless.

Meaning that she was alive. Meaning that the mayor of San Francisco wasn't going to kick their asses around the block after all.

''I killed her?'' Big Mike said. ''You dumb fuckin' bastard. I oughta punch your face in when we get done here.''

Eve moaned again, and Big Mike went back to luring her into full consciousness.

# 23

If you looked carefully at the two Chinese people at the back gate of the large estate, father and daughter, they didn't look quite right.

Was it because their gray clothes didn't fit—the gray pants far too short on the father, the gray jacket far too big on the daughter? Or was it the way their straw hats sloped almost comically low across their faces, as if they wanted to hide? Or the way they grunted and muttered to the gatekeeper's questions, rather than speaking intelligibly, as if they did not want their voices heard?

Fortunately for the two would-be Chinese, the gatekeeper was having problems with his wife at home. His mind was elsewhere. He sensed that there might be something wrong with the two people, but he wasn't interested enough to check them out.

Slocum and Lilly pushed their cart through the opening gate, congratulating themselves on their cleverness.

San Francisco was a city of mansions and wealth, but there were few places that could compare to this one.

The Victorian house came complete with turrets,

spires, and a captain's walk from which you could see the Bay.

As they approached the house, Slocum said, "I wonder if they joust here on Sunday afternoons."

"What's jousting?"

"That's when two knights get on horses and come at each other with lances."

"That sounds like fun."

"As long as you're the winner."

She looked around some more. "This is incredible."

"It certainly is."

"She's not gonna be easy to find."

"I know."

"Let's get rid of this cart and start looking for her."

"Yes, Boss," Slocum said.

Lilly giggled.


"Give her some more water," Big Mike said.

Eve sat up straight now. She took the water gratefully, and took great, deep drinks.

Then she looked up at Big Mike and said, "I don't know where the ledgers are. I really don't."

Big Mike shook his head. "You want me to go back to whuppin' you?"

Rick said, "Go easy, Big Mike."

Big Mike grinned. "I think he's got a crush on you." He looked down at her naked breasts. "Course, I can understand that. You got a real fine body, miss.

"But that won't stop me from doin' what needs to be done," he said. "Gettin' you to tell us where we find those ledgers."

She flushed and dropped her head. "Don't hit me anymore. Please."

"Then you tell us what we need to know."

She felt herself weaken, and in a moment of pain and confusion said, "He always told Father Michaels at the church everything. Ask the Father about the Silver Stallion. That's all I know. Honest."

Rick said, "Maybe she really don't know any more, Big Mike."

"Uh-huh. Now you're startin' to do just what she wants you to. To think that she really don't know where those ledgers are."

Big Mike pulled on the rubber glove he used for the kind of special work this situation required. He went over, stood right in front of Eve, and said, "You want to make this easy for both of us, little lady?"

"I'd like to see my mother."

Big Mike snorted. "Little lady, your mother can't help you now. Haven't you figured that out yet?"

"I'd still like to see her." Eve looked and sounded ten years old. "Please," she said.

Big Mike slapped her, a hard looping slap that lifted her up from her chair and slammed her back against the wall.

Big Mike was about to hit her again when there was a knock on the door.

Rick went over and opened the door a crack.

While he did so, Eve leaned against the wall—where she'd been knocked by Big Mike's blow—and felt the ropes begin to loosen from the impact.

Henry, the mayor of San Francisco, came into the room, looking at Eve and shaking his head.

Both her eyes were blackened. Her lips were cut. Her own blood was spattered on her exposed breasts.

"What the hell have you been doing to her?" the mayor demanded of Big Mike.

"Just what you said," Big Mike said. "Exactly what

you said. Trying to find out where the ledgers are.''

''You had to hit her that hard?''

''I may have to hit her a lot harder. She ain't tellin' us jack shit.''

The mayor was genuinely disturbed by what he saw. Even though he knew he and Belle would never be friends again, he still had some respect for what they'd once been together. He sure as hell didn't want to see her little daughter beaten up.

''I'll talk to her,'' Henry said.

Big Mike smirked. ''Oh, yeah, like she'll listen to you because you're such an important man.''

The mayor nodded to the door. ''You two men wait outside. I'll call you back in when you're needed.''

Big Mike sighed. ''She's knows but she don't want to tell, and there's only one way you're gonna get her to tell.''

He led Rick to the door, then looked back at the mayor. ''Good luck, Henry.''

''I asked you not to call me Henry.''

''Sure thing—Henry.''

Big Mike and Rick both laughed at Big Mike's great grand humor. Then they left the room.

''Some nice friends you've got there,'' Eve said.

''I don't need any more sarcasm today, Eve. I've had quite enough.''

Henry started to pace. ''We have a problem,'' he said.

''*You* have a problem.''

''I need the ledgers back. You had no right to steal them.''

''Have you ever spent any time in Chinatown, Henry? Or over by the Barbary Coast? And looked at all the starving children and women? Or all the shop owners your police extort money from and then kill if they don't come through?''

Given her blackened eyes and battered face, Henry was surprised that Eve could summon so much ire.

"It's going to change, Henry. If these ledgers don't bring you down, something else will. But it's going to change. I promise you.'' She was getting emotional now, sounding as if she were about to cry.

"You realize, of course, that your mother will also get swept out with this new broom?''

"It's time my mother took up a new way of life anyway.''

"You sound very determined.''

"I am, Henry. I am. And I'm also very unforgiving.''

He stopped his pacing and stared at her. "Meaning what?''

"Meaning that you killed Sam Myles.''

"He wasn't what you thought he was, Eve.''

"Yes, he was. Or at least he was trying to be. And that's more than can be said for you.''

Very quietly, he said, "I want those ledgers, Eve.''

"I don't know where they are and if I did, I wouldn't give them to you anyway.''

He took a Peacemaker from inside his coat, walked four steps to her, put the gun to her head, and pulled back the hammer.

"Eve, just please make this easy for me. Where are the ledgers?''

But she didn't speak.

And a moment later, a gunshot reverberated through the house.

# 24

One thing you learned quickly about the house: It had a lot of stairs and a lot of narrow, confusing passage-ways.

A fella could get lost for what seemed years in a place like this.

And now one fella and one young girl, both got up as Chinese folks, were profoundly lost.

They had followed a simple six-step stairway to a door that promised them entrance into the main part of the place.

From there, they reasoned, they would search for Eve, find her, rescue her, and get the hell out.

However, things had not gone so well.

True, they did find the door unlocked. True, they did find a passageway on the other side of the door. And true, from time to time they heard brief volleys of human voices. They were very near the heart of the castle. They were sure of it.

And yet now, after ten sweaty and increasingly frantic minutes, they seemed no closer to the main hallways than they had been at the start.

"Since you're the adult and all, you're in charge, right, Slocum?"

"Right."

"Then where the hell are we?"

"We're in a very short, very narrow passageway that reminds me a lot of a tomb."

"Yeah, kind've reminds me of the same thing," Lilly said. "So, you being the adult and all, how the hell do we get out of here?"

"How old are you?"

"Twelve."

"That's pretty young."

"Asshole."

"You're also too young to talk like that."

"We're lost, aren't we, Slocum?"

"Will you be happier if I say yes?"

"Yes."

"All right, we're lost. Now just what the hell did that accomplish?"

She didn't answer.

They had come to another door at the far end of the narrow, dusty passageway.

"Wanna bet this isn't the right door?" Lilly said.

"I'll bet you a silver dollar it is."

"You're on."

He was just about to reach down and put his hand on the knob when he heard the gunshot.

"What the hell was that?" Slocum said.

He jerked open the door and started running toward the echoing sound of the gunfire.

He was several yards down the hall, his gun in his hand, before he realized that they had indeed found the house's main hall.

Lilly owed him a silver dollar.

# 25

When Belle Kelly heard the shot from down the hall, she ran to the door of the drawing room and fled in the direction of the gunfire.

Young ladies in various stages of undress ran into the halls; the old black servant drew a small derringer from inside his left jacket cuff.

Belle ran to the room where Eve was being questioned.

She grabbed the knob, twisted it, and was surprised to find it open.

She ran inside, saw what had happened, and said, "My God!"

Slocum and Lilly had just rounded the corner leading to the steps to the third floor when they saw a stubby man in a cheap suit, his hand poised as if about to draw his pistol. He stood on the bottom step of the stairway.

"What the hell you two doin' here?"

"So solly, sir," Slocum said, knowing how corny he sounded with the bad Chinese accent. He even gave the thug a little bow. As did Lilly.

When Slocum started to rise up from the bow, he noticed that the thug had finally made the decision to draw his pistol.

It was the wrong decision to make because it forced Slocum to jerk his own pistol from inside his too-tight Chinese jacket and put a bullet right in the thug's forehead.

Lilly grabbed Slocum's gun arm and clung tight to him. "You killed him."

"We'll have to move fast, Lilly. We need to get to the third floor. The dead guy wouldn't have been there if Eve wasn't."

They were already running to the stairs that led to the next floor.

When they reached the dead man, Lilly paused and looked down at him.

"Boy, he's really dead. You got him right in the middle of the forehead, Slocum."

"Yeah." Slocum grinned. "But I was aiming for his shoulder."

"Very funny. Ha-ha. Can't you take a compliment?"

"C'mon, kid, we've got to get going."

They took the stairs two at a time.

They had just reached the top when more gunfire could be heard.

Big Mike and Rick had seen them coming, knew they didn't belong here, and had decided to take care of them.

Slocum and Lilly fled back down the stairs. With both Big Mike and Rick toting shotguns, Slocum and Lilly needed to make some other plans.

Quickly.


Belle Kelly slammed the door behind her and smiled. "Well, I'll be damned. What happened, Henry, did my little girl take your gun away from you?''

Henry sulked, holding on to his biceps where he'd been shot a few moments earlier.

Belle had been so happy to see that Eve was alive, she'd hadn't noticed the black eyes and the bruised cheeks and the torn dress. Not at first. But now she noticed them all.

"Henry did this?'' she asked Eve, who was holding up the tatters of her dress to cover her breasts.

"Not him personally. His two men, Big Mike and Rick.''

"Big Mike and Rick. What a pair they are,'' Belle said.

She walked over and looked at Henry.

"I could get lead poisoning,'' said the mayor.

"You sissy,'' Belle said. "A little flesh wound and you're crying like a baby.''

She slapped him then, so hard that his head jerked back to meet the wall, so hard that his knees started to buckle.

"I owe you big for this, Henry, and I'm going to keep my word too. You're going to die for what you did to my daughter, but first you're going to suffer. One way or another, I'm going to find those ledgers and then I'm going to turn them over to the newspapers and watch your fine fancy family be humiliated. That'll be even worse than death for them, that kind of scandal, Henry. And you know just who they'll blame too, don't you? Little Henry, their ne'er-do-well son.''

She had just started to call him names when the unfamiliar sound of gunfire once again echoed off the pristine walls of this spacious and magnificent place.

•　•　•

There was a back staircase in the place that wound through the east part of the house.

Once Slocum and Lilly found it, they had no trouble reaching the third floor again.

Slocum eased the door open and peeked out.

Big Mike and Rick had their backs to Slocum now.

Slocum said, "Boys, if you put those guns down right now without any hassle, everything's gonna be fine. But if you don't, I'll blow your fucking heads off. You understand me."

"Shit," Big Mike said.

"That sumbitch," Rick said.

"Snuck up on us," Big Mike said.

"That asshole," said Rick.

"I said to put your guns down."

"Sumbitch," Rick said again, and that was when he whirled and tried to squeeze off a quick blast with his shotgun.

But he was too slow.

Slocum put a bullet into the floor at Rick's feet.

Rick froze.

Big Mike and Rick slowly set their shotguns down. Then they raised their arms.

Lilly came out of the door behind Slocum.

"Let's go get Eve," Slocum said.

# 26

But the shooting wasn't over yet.

From the far end of the hall, barely visible from where Slocum stood, another man—this one with a rifle instead of the usual shotgun—peeked around the corner and fired off three rounds aimed at Slocum.

Big Mike and Rick hit the ground for cover, as did Lilly.

Slocum stood still, squeezing off two shots at the rifleman.

He wasn't being heroic. There just wasn't any good place to hide.

The hallway was tart with gunsmoke.

You could hear everybody breathing, fear making them breathe fast and shallow, each of them—Lilly, Big Mike, and Rick—making little animal mewls of anxiety, probably even unaware they were making them.

Slocum felt the anxiety too, his bowels tight, sweat pooling in his armpits and on the soles of his feet.

The rifleman did not show his face again for a good minute and a half. If nothing else, he was a patient bastard.

Slocum eased the hammer back on his weapon.

Sighted. Steadied his hand.

Waited.

The rifleman might have been a jack-in-the-box, given how his face suddenly popped up again, all beard grizzle and stupidly grinning.

He got a shot off, but not as quickly as Slocum did. Nor as accurately.

The jack-in-the-box face changed suddenly. The nose exploded right at the bridge, right at the bullet's point of entry. The eyes went wide with shock and terror, too blue and too big, and then the mouth began gushing blood.

No, the rifleman had lost his jack-in-the-box look altogether.

He stood there for a long moment, letting all these terrible things happen to his face, and then he went over backwards.

He squeezed off a dying shot, but it went directly and uselessly into the ceiling.

"C'mon," Slocum said to Lilly, "let's get Eve."

There had been a time when Detective Halliwell had enjoyed coming to the station house and having a cigar and a cup of coffee with the other coppers before starting his duties.

But this was before he'd realized, in his somewhat naive way, that the other coppers were not like him.

The other coppers were thieves, arsonists, extortionists, and even murderers.

The other coppers paid no allegiance to the Constitution of the United States or the Bill of Rights or the Policeman's Code as it had been adopted in New York last year.

No, his fellow officers paid allegiance to only one man, the mayor of San Francisco, a weak and hopelessly corrupt man.

Girls, gambling, booze, violence—you could get any of it in the places from which the mayor skimmed his twenty-percent extortion money. And God help you if you tried to run your business without the approval of the mayor.

Just ask the man whose head had been found bobbing in the Bay one fine sunny May morning.

Now Detective Halliwell stood at his desk and looked at the faces, young and old, smart and dumb, handsome and ugly, and wondered how they could live this sham. How could they spend their entire lives pretending to be something they weren't?

"Captain wants to see you, Halliwell," Detective Kirk said as he passed quickly by.

Nobody stayed long at Halliwell's desk. Nobody invited the Halliwells over for dinner. Nobody asked Halliwell to play on the policemen's baseball team.

He was marked queer for his old-fashioned beliefs in honor and justice, and in fact most of his fellow officers looked on him with astonishment. How had he managed to stay alive all these years? Given his refusal to take bribe money, he was lucky somebody hadn't killed him by now.

Captain Fallon was waiting for him, still in his office despite the late hour.

"Got kind of curious where you've been lately, Halliwell."

"Doing my job, sir."

"Your job as you see it or as I see it?"

"I guess as I see it, sir."

"That's what I thought." Fallon leaned back in his

office chair, tapping a pencil on the edge of his desk. He was a slender, nervous, balding man. There was always a certain frantic air about him, as if he knew that the end of the world was coming soon and he wanted to get everything wrapped up before it did. Under other circumstances, Halliwell might even have liked the man. But Fallon was so corrupt, liking him was impossible. He'd been wrong so many years he could never be right again.

"I wanted you down on the docks yesterday, Halliwell."

"I know that, sir."

"Those union bastards are trying to organize the men again."

Halliwell nodded. "I know you don't like to hear this, sir, but that's their right. It's perfectly legal, trying to organize those men."

Fallon smirked. "I should start sending you around to grade schools in the Bay area. You could give talks on civics."

Halliwell flushed. Anger he could handle, but not being mocked.

Fallon sat up and tossed the pencil on his cluttered desk.

"I've been told you're still looking for some ledgers that were taken from the mayor."

Halliwell said nothing.

"This is where you're going to get killed, Halliwell. I hope you know that. You've been fucking around on the edges for a long time, waging your little one-man cleanup campaign, and nobody's bothered you because you weren't worth bothering with. But this is different, Halliwell. You understand?"

"I understand."

Fallon grinned. "A smart guy, he got his hands on those ledgers, you know what he'd do with 'em?"

"What, sir?"

"He'd sell them back to the mayor for a lot of money."

"That isn't what I had in mind."

"Oh, I know that, Halliwell. I know what a decent, churchgoing man you are. No, sir, Halliwell gets his hands on those ledgers, no way he'd do anything like shake the mayor down with them. Oh, no, not true-blue Halliwell. He'll take them right to the newspapers and they'll bring the mayor down, right, Halliwell?"

"Something like that."

"Well, let me tell you something, Halliwell. You try something like that, not only are you dead but so is your family. Your wife and your new son."

"How do you know about him already?"

"Certain people have taken a great interest in you lately, Halliwell. They're watching you closely. Very closely." The smirk again. "I just thought maybe you'd like to know that."

"I appreciate the tip."

"It doesn't scare you?"

"Of course it scares me."

"Then you'll forget about those ledgers?"

Halliwell sighed. "Wouldn't you like to live in a clean town, Fallon? Where people had respect for the coppers because the coppers had earned their respect?"

Fallon laughed. "I'm definitely gonna send you out to give civics lessons to grade school kids, Halliwell. I really think you missed your calling."

# 27

"Gimme."

"Huh?"

"Gimme." Lilly put out her hand, palm up.

"Give you what?" Slocum said.

"That extra gun. The one you took from the mayor."

"For what?"

"For me. For protection."

"You're a kid."

"Kids don't need protection?"

They were still in the drawing room where Eve had been held. The violence of the past few hours was reflected in the overturned furniture.

Slocum sighed. "I know you'd like a gun, Lilly, but it just isn't a good idea."

"You don't trust me, huh?"

"It's just your age."

Lilly looked up at him. "If I ask you a question, will you be honest?"

"This is a trick question, right?"

"No trick question. All I want to know is if you'll answer honest."

He smiled down at her elfin face. "I'll answer honest."

"How old were you when you got your first gun?"

"No fair."

"What's that supposed to mean?"

"No fair. Because I grew up out in the wide outdoors where you needed a gun."

"The city's a lot more dangerous than the wide outdoors ever was." She looked up at him again. "How old were you?"

"Nine."

"See?"

"But it's different. When I was nine I . . ."

She grinned. She had him and she knew it. And he knew it.

She put her hand out again. Palm up. "C'mon, Slocum. Gimme the gun."

"You're a devil, you know that?"

"C'mon, Slocum, the gun."

He shook his head. "A real little devil, you know that?"

She laughed. "Yeah, and you love it, Slocum."

He gave her the gun.

# 28

Getting Eve out of the mansion wasn't as easy as Slocum had hoped.

After finding Eve some new clothes, after tying up Big Mike and Rick, after checking the stairways and doors for signs of any other henchmen, Slocum took the mayor as a hostage and moved down the three flights of stairs to the front door.

"Make sure we're clear outside," Slocum said to Lilly, who ran through the front door eagerly, her Peacemaker steady in her hand, ready to fire whenever necessary.

Front porch and yard were clear.

"Everything's fine," she said.

"You're going to regret this," the mayor said.

"I don't think so," Slocum said. "We're going to find those ledgers and then we're going to watch them hang you."

"You're very confident, now," the mayor said. "But just wait till the manhunt goes into effect. Shoot on sight will be the order, Slocum. Shoot on sight."

"Say good-bye to everybody," Slocum said. "You're

going to take a nice little nap for yourself.''

And with that, he hit the mayor directly on the temple, reducing the tall man to a heap in the doorway.

Eve leaned over and kissed Belle Kelly on the cheek. ''Aren't you afraid of him, Mother?''

She smiled. ''Not anymore, I'm not.''

''But when he comes to . . .''

''You and Slocum here just go find those ledgers. That's all you should be worried about now. You understand?''

While the two women embraced, Slocum dragged the mayor's body back inside. The mayor was already groaning his way back to consciousness. ''You bastard,'' he said, peering up at Slocum through painful eyes.

''Next time I'm going to beat you up just the way you had Eve beat up. Then we'll see how you like it.''

Then he raised his gun and brought the barrel down along the side of the mayor's head again. ''Sweet dreams, asshole,'' Slocum said.

He stood up and went back to the two ladies. ''You about ready, Eve?''

She nodded and kissed her mother quickly again.

Lilly frowned. ''Hell, I thought for sure I would get to use my gun this time.''

Slocum laughed. ''I'm sure you'll have plenty of opportunity for some gunplay, kiddo. This isn't over by a long shot.''

''I'm holding you responsible for my daughter's well-being, Mr. Slocum,'' Belle Kelly said.

''She'll be fine,'' Slocum said, though he admitted to some doubts.

The mayor hadn't been exaggerating about a manhunt. He'd have no problem bringing out a couple thousand Bay area men to look for Slocum. No problem at all. And every one of them would be eager to pull the trigger, eager to say he was the one who killed Big Bad Slocum.

Hell, that was the sort of thing that got you in the *The Police Gazette*.

"Look," Lilly said.

"What?"

"Across the street."

Slocum looked. "I'll be damned," he said.

"Still following us around. Who the hell is he?"

"That's what I'd like to know," Slocum said. "But right now there isn't time to find out."

Belle came over and squinted. "Mighty fancy dresser whoever he is," she said.

"Nice new suit," Slocum said.

"Real fine walking stick," Lilly said. "How long you reckon he's been following you?"

"Ever since your father got killed."

He saw pain freeze Lilly for a moment. It was easy to forget, what with her rough language and rougher attitude, that here was a very young girl who—despite all her efforts to hide the fact—was very sensitive to the death of her father.

Slocum eased her to him and gave her a fatherly kiss on top of the head.

"We're not only going to find out who that man is over there, Lilly," he said, "we're also going to find out which one of the mayor's men killed your father. Then we're gonna take care of him personally."

"You promise, Slocum?"

"I promise."

Eve smiled at Lilly. "And I make the same promise,

Lilly. I know how much you love him—and I know how much he loved you."

"C'mon," Slocum said. "Let's go find that priest who was Sam's friend. Maybe he can help us with the ledgers."

# 29

Slocum wasn't sure how to make the sign of the cross, so all he did when they got inside the church was take off his Stetson and sort of nod in the direction of the altar.

The church, with its vaulting nave, its gentle smell of incense, and its long shadows, was actually a restful place.

Lilly—who was, incredibly enough, a churchgoer—went to look for Father Michaels, leaving Eve and Slocum in a front pew.

"They're so pretty."

"Huh?" Slocum said.

"The stained-glass windows with the sunlight behind them."

"Oh. Yeah. Right."

Eve smiled. Even with her black eyes, she was pretty. "You ever thought of giving it up, Slocum?"

"Giving what up?"

"You know. All the craziness. The women and the violence and the drifting."

"You make me sound like a real nice guy."

"You are. In your own very special way anyway. Sam was like that. A great guy—once you understood the terms he lived on."

"Right now, all I'm worried about is finding those ledgers. We owe it to Sam."

"We sure do. I just hope I can get my mother out of San Francisco if we ever find them. I have a feeling His Honor the Mayor will want to take everybody down with him, including my mother."

"You leave Henry to me," Slocum said. "I'll take care of that sonofabitch."

"Go a little easy on the language, Slocum. We're in church."

She smiled and touched his hand, and he had to admit that it was nice be touched so gently by somebody you respected.

Maybe someday he would quit all this craziness after all.

Lilly came back accompanied by a squat nun. She looked like a waddling penguin.

"This is Sister Anne."

Slocum stood up and gave her a little bow.

The sister gave him a little bow right back.

"I'm afraid that Father Michaels is at the hospital right now giving a dying man the last rites."

"Know when he'll be back?"

"A few hours, I would think," the nun said.

"All right, Sister. We'll try him then."

But the nun wasn't finished. "It's about the ledgers, isn't it?"

"Mind if I ask how you knew that?" Slocum said.

"Because the mayor also sent a man this afternoon looking for Father Michaels." She shook her head.

"There's going to be bad trouble in this city tonight. I can feel it."

Slocum automatically brushed his hand against his holster, his way of agreeing with the nun about trouble tonight.

"Thank you, Sister. We'll be back in a while."

"I'll be praying for you."

"We appreciate that, Sister," Eve said.

"Yeah, Sister," Lilly said, "we really do."

The nun nodded and walked back down the long center aisle.

At the altar, she got down on one knee and crossed herself.

Then she stood up and left the church by a side door.

"C'mon," Slocum said.

"Where we going?" Lilly asked.

"Your dad's office. Maybe there's something there we overlooked."

# 30

"I thought you were going to kill me."

The mayor of San Francisco stood in the doorway of Belle Kelly's bedroom trying to sound sardonic and self-confident.

He simply sounded, as usual, foolish.

Belle was packing. She had a large trunk set up open on her bed beneath the frilly canopy of blue silk.

The mayor of San Francisco had taken her many times in this bed, and he was thinking of that now. He knew for sure that he had truly loved her—maybe the only woman he had ever truly loved—but he had never felt that she had loved him.

"I had to do it, Belle. To Eve, I mean. They—they're very angry men, Belle. They'll kill me if I don't get those ledgers back."

She raised her head and looked at him. At first she was angry—he looked so weak and lost. He needed a nanny. And seeing that, she was angry no longer. She was simply sad. For him, for herself, for Eve. She was sick of her life, and sick of her vanity, and she just wanted to be done with it, go somewhere and be nobody, and live out her days with at least a modicum of self-respect and peace of mind. All her life she had craved excitement—craved the glamour of the high life—but she was through with it now, and through with all the weak, foolish men who went along with it.

"Maybe they'd be doing you a favor, Henry."

"A favor? By killing me?"

She sighed. "Maybe you'd better do what I'm going to."

"And what's that?"

"Leave."

"Leave the city?"

"Yes."

"When?"

"Now. Right now, Henry. And for good."

"What about Eve?"

"She'll be all right now. Slocum will take care of her—and do a lot better job of it than I could."

"I feel like crying, Belle. Like just sitting down and goddamn bawling. I don't know how things could ever have gotten as fucked up as they are."

"No," Belle said, finishing packing, closing the lid of the trunk. "I sure don't know they ever got this fucked up either, Henry."

# 31

The city was dark and quiet as Slocum, Lilly, and Eve reached the building where Sam Myles had kept his office.

When she saw the place, Eve said, "I remember the day he saw this place. How proud he was. He said, 'I'm going to be a real businessman now. A reputable private investigator.' " She seemed to laugh and cry at the same time. "He was just like a little boy."

She reached over, pulled Lilly to her, and gave her a hug. "And I know that he would have just loved having you with him. He would have been proud to show you that you had a respectable father after all."

Slocum smiled. "He really had changed, hadn't he?"

"Oh, yes," Eve said. "Even if people didn't want to believe it, it was true."

As they climbed the stairs to Myles's office, they heard from the waterfront the lonely call of a tugboat, sounding like a prehistoric beast lost on the fog-bound sea.

When they got to Myles's office, Slocum said, "If you don't have the key, Eve, I can just pick the lock."

Eve looked at Lilly and smiled. "The next guy who needs to give up his shady past and go straight is our friend Slocum here."

Detective Halliwell wasn't sure when the two men started following him, but there they were, keeping a discreet quarter block away.

He decided to have a little fun with them.

Once they all got out of the business area, he led them to the city barns, where the street-cleaning department kept all its vehicles.

The barn Halliwell chose was huge. Only a little moonlight came in through a broken skylight. Just enough shadows for him to hide in. Just enough light for him to see.

When he was sure they were watching him closely, he went up to one of the big sliding doors, eased it open, and then got inside.

Outside he left two very perplexed shadows.

Why the hell was Halliwell going inside a city barn? That was the first question.

The second question was: Should they risk going after him inside?

Which led, inevitably, to the third question. Was he aware of them and coyly leading them into a trap?

Sometimes it was very difficult to know what to do in this vale of tears.

You had to take real risks, and that could mean really getting your ass kicked around the block.

But these two were bruisers, six-one and six-three respectively, with a combined weight of 523 pounds, and more than two hundred knockouts to their credit—not in boxing rings, but in alleys, saloons, and billiard parlors.

So what the hell . . .

There were two of them and one of him.

How scary could it get?

Well, actually, pretty scary.

For one thing, the inside of the barn was *dark*. It took a while for their eyes to adjust, and the two kept accidentally bumping into each other like a bad vaudeville act. For another thing, they couldn't find a lantern anywhere. They felt around on the walls like a couple of blind guys desperately looking for a door, but . . . nothing.

And for a third thing, Halliwell had in fact coyly and blithely and proudly led them into a trap . . . and a real good one.

Here were the two of them innocently standing in the middle of the vast open area between the sides of the barn when Halliwell, up above them on the right side of the loft, let fly with a heavy steel winch at the end of a long rope that . . .

Well, it was sort of like bowling.

Here came the winch flying through the air. There stood the two unsuspecting shadows. The winch and a human head met, and the sound was sort of like a splat when the first guy's head burst open.

Then there were other sounds immediately. The surviving member of the duo had a pretty dirty mouth on him, and used it to fill the entire interior of the barn with every epithet known to critters that walked on two legs.

This only helped the industrious Halliwell, of course.

True, he could see a little bit in the moonlight, but he could hear even better.

So after he grabbed the rope and brought the winch back—now dripping with blood and fuzzy with hair and shimmering with liver-like pieces of brain—he just listened carefully to the foul-mouth below him and honed in accordingly.

He let the winch swing right to where the dirty words were coming from.

Again, the satisfying sound of a splat. A body crumpled to the floor.

Halliwell smiled to himself, the satisfied smile of a man who works hard at what he does and takes pride in his accomplishments.

He scrambled down the ladder and went over to the dead men. They'd filled their pants, so they weren't exactly what you'd call great dinner companions.

He gingerly removed their wallets from their back pockets and carried them outside the door, to use the moonlight for reading.

He found exactly what he'd expected to find. These two fine specimens—well, previously fine specimens— had been San Francisco police officers.

Halliwell had no doubt now what he was up against.

His own fellow officers meant to kill him, just as they'd killed officers in the past who'd tried to clean up the department.

Shaking his head, he took the two wallets over to a wide, deep garbage can and threw them in.

Might as well make the coppers do a little extra work in trying to identify the two dead men.

Then Halliwell was on his way again. He walked eight blocks north of his destination just to see if anybody else had picked him up yet. Sometimes surveillance people worked in teams. If one got lost or put out of commission, then the other one took over.

But he found nobody.

On all sides of him now the San Francisco night was

alive, laughter and curses and drunken chatter filling the air.

But for Halliwell there would be no time for pleasure tonight.

Now that he was free of tails, he had to set about the business of finding the ledgers and bringing down the mayor of the beautiful city by the Bay.

# 32

Big Mike and Rick sat in the same church that Slocum and his friends had inhabited less than an hour ago. Like Slocum, they were waiting to see Father Michaels.

"My ass is goin' to sleep," Big Mike said.

"I don't think you should say that so loud in here, Big Mike," Rick said.

"Aw, bullshit."

"Ya never know." Rick nodded solemnly toward the altar. "I mean, if He's listen' He might get pissed—er, mad. Ya know?"

Big Mike frowned. He wanted, in no particular order, a steak, a woman, a good poker hand, and a face to punch in. His were the simple pleasures.

"They're pretty," Rick said.

"Huh?"

"Them candles. All them different colors."

"The votive candles, you mean."

"How come they call 'em votive? What do candles have to do with voting?"

"How the fuck should I know?"

"Yer swearin' again, Big Mike. I really don't think

you should do that in here.''

"Just sit there and shut up.''

"Maybe he won't be back till midnight. That priest, I mean.''

"You hear what I said?''

"Yeah. I heard ya.''

"Then shut up.''

"Nobody said you could boss me around.''

"I said I could.''

Rick knew he'd pushed it as far as he could. He spent at least a quarter of his waking hours irritating Big Mike. And Big Mike was too stupid to understand that he was being irritated on purpose.

Big Mike was so stupid he figured that Rick was the stupid one.

But you always reached a point with Big Mike. Beyond that point, you didn't push. Not if you wanted to live to a decent old age.

"I don't want ya t'hum either,'' Big Mike said after a time.

"I wasn't hummin'.''

"Hell you weren't. You hum half the time yer awake. Drives me fuckin' batty.''

"What do I hum?''

"All kinds of shit.''

Big Mike was just about to say more when he heard the back door of the huge church open, heard quick footsteps come up to the main floor, and then heard a man cough somewhere in the candle-flickering shadows of the place.

Then Big Mike saw him.

Father Michaels. All got up in his black cassock and white Roman collar.

The priest who had been helping Sam Myles go

straight. The priest whose name they had just learned about today. The priest who might well lead them to the ledgers.

Big Mike stood up and said, "Father?" His voice echoed off the vaulted ceilings and the walls with the Stations of the Cross painted on them.

"You must be the man my housekeeper told me about," Father Michaels said. He came over, a small, trim, quick man beginning to lose his hair at age forty.

"I'm Big Mike and this is Rick."

"Hello, Rick."

The priest offered his hand. The men shook.

"Now, how can I help you men?"

"Friend of ours meant us to get something in case he ever died, but unfortunately we was out of town when he passed away and so we didn't get it."

Father Michaels said, "Was this friend of yours a member of our parish here?"

"I think he was, Father."

"What was his name?"

"Sam Myles."

Big Mike couldn't be quite sure what it was, but a change came over Father Michaels with the mention of Sam's name. The priest seemed to become tight, suspicious.

"So Sam was a friend of yours?"

"Yes, Father, he was."

"How long had you known him?"

"Ten years," Big Mike said.

"Then you must have known him when he lived up on the Russian River."

"Uh, yeah."

"Good friends even back then, huh?"

"Very good friends. The best."

"You know something, Big Mike?"

"What, Father?"

"Sam Myles never lived up on the Russian River."

"You know something, Father?"

"What?"

"I don't give a shit where Sam Myles lived."

And with that, he brought up his .45 and placed it right against the small priest's temple.

"Now we're gonna have ourselves a nice little confession here, Father." Big Mike looked over at Rick and winked. "You're gonna confess to me where I can find them ledgers Sam Myles had."

# 33

"Was he handsome, Eve?"

"Very handsome."

"Was he fun to be around?"

"A lot of fun."

"Was he nice?"

"Very nice. Very nice."

"I wish I coulda known him."

"I wish you could've known him too, Lilly."

Slocum, Lilly, and Eve had been in Sam Myles's office for nearly half an hour now.

While Slocum fastidiously went through all the desk drawers, all the filing cabinet drawers, and all the loose papers in a small box next to the desk, Eve and Lilly sat outside the closet sorting through a box of letters they'd found in there.

"Any luck, Slocum?" Eve said.

"Not so far. You?"

"Not so far either."

They went back to their searching.

"Did he like to dance, Eve?" Lilly asked.

"He loved to dance."

"Was he good?"

"He was great."

"Did he dress up when he took you dancin'?"

"He dressed up real fine."

"Boiled white shirt?"

"Boiled white shirt and sharp blue suit and fine shiny black shoes."

"My ma always said he was one of the handsomest men she ever saw."

"She was right, Lilly. She was absolutely right."

"I wish I could have danced with him."

"I know, hon."

"And I sure wish I could've seen him in his sharp blue suit."

"Aw, hon," Eve said tenderly, and started to give the young girl a hug.

"Hot shit," said Slocum, which kind of spoiled the sentimental mood of the moment. "Look what I found."

# 34

Father Michaels said, "I don't know where the ledgers are."

Big Mike looked around the church. "Wonder how loud a gunshot in here would be? Probably break your eardrums."

Shadows cast by the flickering votive candles moved like sylphs across the stone walls of the vast church.

"Maybe you should go a little easy," Rick said, "him bein' a priest and all."

Big Mike grabbed Father Michaels and hurled him into a pew.

The priest sprawled across the seat and struggled to get up.

"Go get the housekeeper," Big Mike said.

"Huh?"

"You heard me, Rick. I said to get the housekeeper."

"Aw, Big Mike, listen . . ."

Big Mike grabbed Rick now and gave him a hard shove down the center aisle. "You heard what I said."

• • •

Sure and hadn't she come over from Dublin only ten years ago, a whole decade now that Mary Greene had been an American?

Sure and didn't she have the best American job of them all, enjoying the riches and freedoms of this country while working for the priests, which meant being about as close to God as you could get in this vale of tears.

Now, as she washed the dishes in the rectory's kitchen, she hummed an ancient Irish ballad to herself, "The Ship on the Midnight Sea," a haunting tune that her Grandfather McGill used to sing to her when time rolled round for all little girls to be in bed.

Even here, in the nice, clean, white kitchen—so typical of all the nice, clean, white things in this brand-new land—even in America the tune kept its moody charms.

She was just about to pour a little more hot water on the dishes when she heard something at the side door behind her.

When she turned to look, she saw a rough-looking man in a cheap suit and an almost-comic bowler standing there.

"Beggin' yer pardon, ma'am."

"Yes?"

Like most men, Rick sensed at once that here was a very strong woman. "I, uh, come t'fetch ya."

"Fetch me, is it? And for what, might I ask?"

"So you can go help Father Michaels."

"Help him? What're you talkin' about?" Mary said. Her stomach started to tighten, her pulse to race. Of all the four priests here, Father Michaels was surely her favorite. She knew that was a wrong-headed, maybe even sinful attitude—all priests, just like all people, being equal in God's eyes—but she couldn't help it. She liked Father Michaels's boyishness, his little jokes, his little remembrances of her birthday and Christmas and Easter.

She wiped her hands on a towel. "Where is he?"

"In the church."

"And he's been injured?"

"Ya better just come along, I guess."

"And who're you to be orderin' me about this way?" Then she saw the gun in his hand. "Who are you anyway?"

"Don't matter, ma'am. You just come with me."

"If I were my father or any of my six brothers, I'd slap that stupid face of yours and take that gun away and make you eat it."

"No call for gettin' so riled up."

"No call? You come into a holy place like a rectory—not as holy as a church, I grant you, but holy nonetheless—and brandish about a weapon of violence, and you tell me not to get riled up?

"Have you never heard of blasphemy, you stupid oaf? That's just what you're doin' here, even if ya don't know—yer blasphemin'!"

"C'mon now. Otherwise Big Mike'll start to hurt him."

"To hurt a consecrated priest?" She had never been so shocked in her life. But the shock finally persuaded her that this situation was not one she could control, even with her fine lashing Dublin tongue, and that Father Michaels really was in some kind of mortal trouble, and that all she could do was go to him and hope she could help him in some way.

"C'mon, now," Rick said.

And so, finally, she relented and went to the church.

• • •

What did you find?'' Eve asked Slocum.

"This,'' he said, and handed over a piece of paper.

On it, written in pencil rather than pen, thus indicating a first draft, were several lines that read:

In case of my death, I want the proper authorities to be given four ledgers given to me by a friend. The ledgers will demonstrate just how corrupt our city government has become. One person, other than myself, knows where these ledgers are being kept. His name is Father Richard Michaels.

There was more. Eve scanned it quickly.

"You were right,'' Slocum said "I thought maybe the priest would turn out not to know anything either. Now we've got to find him.''

Slocum went to the window and looked out on the night.

Below him, San Francisco sprawled beautifully against the hills and night sky.

He looked down at the square below him.

In the soft lamplight, the streets and the square itself looked so beautiful they belonged in a painting. Everything from the haberdashery to the bank with the statue of a horse to the bookstore with the name SHAKE-SPEARE on it looked handsome.

He looked out into the night, trying to see the church from there.

"Maybe we should walk over to the church,'' Eve said, "and see if Father Michaels is back.''

"That's what I was thinking.''

Lilly said, "They must've been good friends, the way my dad trusted this priest.''

"Well, when you've got most of city government and

the police force taking bribes, about the only people you can trust are the clergy.''

Eve and Lilly joined him at the window.

Slocum was still staring below at the square. Something he'd just seen bothered him, but he wasn't sure what . . .

But whatever the thought had been, he'd lost it.

''C'mon,'' he said, ''let's go check on Father Michaels.''

# 35

Halliwell knew the best way to encourage a newspaper man. Find a nice dark bar and keep feeding him whiskey.

The name of the pub was The Alabaster Angel, and the name of the newspaper man was Sullivan.

"So it doesn't mean anything to you?"

"Not right off. But if I sit here long enough..." Sullivan grinned.

"And I put enough whiskeys in your belly."

"With beer chasers as we call them," Sullivan reminded him.

"Then you just might be able to remember...."

Sullivan shrugged. "I hate to come clean on you, Halliwell, especially with the prospect of so many free whiskeys, but at the moment it doesn't mean a damned thing to me."

"The Silver Stallion," Halliwell said.

"The Silver Stallion," Sullivan repeated.

Sullivan was fifty-three years old. For thirty-one of those years he'd been a reporter here in the Bay area.

He knew virtually everybody, every place, every last stray piece of gossip.

But this Silver Stallion business had him stumped. "This is damned hard."

"I thought it might be, Sullivan. That's why I brought so much money along. To buy plenty of drinks."

"And there's no other clue?"

"No other clue. All he said was, 'The Silver Stallion is protecting those ledgers.' I stood outside his office one night and heard him talking to Father Michaels. Twice Myles mentioned this Silver Stallion, but he never said what it was."

"I'll be damned. I'm drawin' a complete blank."

Halliwell shook his head and stood up.

"Yer leavin'?" Sullivan said.

"Empty my bladder."

"Oh."

"You just sit here and think."

"And drink, if you don't mind."

"Oh. Right. And drink."

Sullivan grinned. "If I run out before you get back, I'll order another and charge it to you."

Halliwell laughed. "I thought you might do something like that."

When he got back, four minutes later, he found Sullivan with a fresh drink but a baffled expression.

"Nothing?"

"Nothing yet," Sullivan said.

"Shit," Halliwell said, and sat down.

# 36

In his time, Big Mike had killed somebody in just about every line of work: businessman, laborer, gambler, politician, outlaw.

But he had never killed a member of the clergy before.

He was hoping that the woman Rick was just now pushing up the center aisle of the vast and shadowy church would make that unnecessary.

Rick held a gun to the woman's back as they came down the aisle. "Here's the lady."

Big Mike grabbed her and put his gun to her head. "We're gonna find out just how much the father here likes you, lady."

Father Michaels looked at her and said, "Just say prayers, Mary. This'll all turn out all right. I'm sure of it."

"I'm scared, Father."

"I know, Mary. But you have to have faith in God."

She nodded, ashamed of herself for displaying such cowardice and lack of trust in the Lord.

"Father," she said.

"Yes, Mary?"

"Let him shoot me."

Big Mike laughed. "A real noble lady, ain't ya?"

He reached in front of her and grabbed one of her breasts. "You got a real nice pair for a lady yer age."

"Take your hand off her," Father Michaels said.

"Brave little bantam priest, eh, Mary?"

But he took his hand away.

"All right, Father. I want you to tell me where the ledgers are."

"I've already told you. I don't know."

Big Mike eased the hammer back on his gun. "You probably don't think I'd kill her, do you?"

"I would hope not anyway."

"Well, Father, I've got news for you. I'll kill her in the next ten seconds if you don't tell me what 'The Silver Stallion' means."

"I wouldn't know."

"And after I kill her, then I kill you, Father."

Father Michaels glanced around the church; he wasn't sure what to do. He certainly didn't want to see Mary harmed. But he also didn't want to tell Big Mike what "The Silver Stallion" meant. If those ledgers were returned to the mayor, the city would remain hopelessly corrupt.

"I'm counting, Father. Ten . . ."

And it was then that Father Michaels saw his one and only chance for freedom—and for Mary's survival.

Two feet to his right stood a large, gold-encrusted dish of holy water supported by a large marble stand, a gift from one of the wealthier parishioners.

If he could ease over to it, grab the dish, and temporarily blind Big Mike . . .

"Eight . . . seven . . ."

Father Michaels looked at the fear and torment on Mary's face. Her eyes were closed. She had probably never prayed this hard in her entire life.

"Five . . ."

Father Michaels moved over half a foot, another half a foot, another—

"Three . . ."

Father Michaels reached behind him, brought the bowl up from its resting place, gripped it as best he could with the palm of his hand, and . . .

"Two . . ."

And heaved it in the face of Big Mike.

Just as the bowl struck the outlaw in the face, Father Michaels kicked his right leg up at Big Mike's gun arm, knocking the pistol out of the killer's fingers.

"Run, Mary!" Father Michaels cried out as he started running to the back of the church and to the stairs that led to the choir loft.

Mary obeyed, running up the aisle, then ducking into one of the pews and crawling down beneath the seats, hiding.

Rick fired two shots at the back of the retreating priest, but the gunfire had been intended only to impress Big Mike.

Rick didn't really want to shoot a priest.

He didn't want to burn in eternal flames.

Big Mike recovered himself, picked up his weapon, and started running off after Father Michaels.

"No way he's gonna ever leave this church alive," Big Mike said to himself as he started climbing the stairs to the choir loft. "No, sir. He ain't gonna ever leave this church again."

He moved up the stairs two at a time, trying not to notice how fast and shallow and painful his breath was coming.

He was having too much fun tracking down the priest.

# 37

Sullivan was on his sixth whiskey.

"You don't feel any of those yet?" Detective Halliwell said.

"Hell, Halliwell, you forget. I'm Irish. And a member of the press."

"Oh."

"This ain't nothin'."

"I sure wish you could think of what 'The Silver Stallion' means."

"It'll come to me."

"When?"

"Soon. In the meantime . . ."

Halliwell signaled for two more whiskeys for Sullivan.

"I was just remembering when we first met," Sullivan said. "We were both so full of shit, we were."

"I don't think being idealistic is the same as full of shit."

Sullivan smiled. "Idealistic. God, weren't we, though? You were gonna catch all the crooks and I was gonna write all the truth."

Halliwell couldn't help but be a little sentimental. "I wish I still had some of that innocence."

"Me too."

"Now that I know what most public officials are really like," Halliwell said, "it's hard to have much faith in government." His face grew tight and angry. "That's why those ledgers are so important. They could change everything in this city." He laughed, grabbed one of Sullivan's two whiskeys, and poured the shot down his old gullet. "Oh, for the old days when all we had to worry about were muggers and thieves and bank robbers and—"

"That's it!" Sullivan said, so loudly that everybody in the saloon stopped their conversations and looked over at him.

"What's it?" Halliwell said in the sudden silence.

"Bank robbers."

"What about them?"

"That's where the Silver Stallion is."

"Where?"

"The bank."

And Sullivan, who had just now earned his drinks and a whole hell of a lot more of them besides, told Halliwell not only what the Silver Stallion was but where he could find it.

# 38

Father Michaels could hear Big Mike working his way up the stairs to the choir loft. The stout man's breath came in hard shallow gasps.

The loft was in deep darkness except for a single partially open window where starlight shone.

Father Michaels knelt between the large pipe organ and the steps that led to the belfry. His own breath was coming as quickly as Big Mike's. For all his faith in the Almighty, which was considerable, the human part of the priest was still scared. Only the rare human being really wants to die. Even those who believe completely in the prospect of an afterlife feel some trepidation about reaching the next world.

So the priest waited. And listened. And prepared himself to scurry away once again if need be.

*Gonna beat his fuckin' face in. Gonna take that friggin' Roman collar of his an' gonna put it where the sun don't shine.*

*Sissy fucker. Makin' me climb all them stairs and then gettin' up here and can't see shit.*

*Oh, yeah, gonna waste this fucker real bad once he tells me what I want to know.*

Hail Mary full of grace. Our Father Who art in heaven. Bless me, Father, for I have sinned.

The priest could hear Big Mike getting closer, closer.

So he closed his eyes and said some prayers. Fervent, even desperate prayers.

*Where'd that little pecker go? Gotta be up here somewhere.*

*Sumbitch. Near tripped over them hymnbooks on the floor.*

*Aw, man, I'm gonna beat his ass bloody, that little queer, when I get my hands on him.*

So close he could smell Big Mike now.

So close Big Mike's short gasping breathing was like drumbeats.

So close he could hear the hammer ease back on Big Mike's gun.

*That organ. Gotta be. Only place he could possibly be hidin'. I've checked everyplace else up here.*

*Little prick.*

*It's all over for ya. All friggin' over.*

The gunshot roared like a cosmic storm, echoing off ceiling and walls and floors, driving Father Michaels from his hiding spot, sending him frantically to the ladder that led to the belfry.

Big Mike would have a clear shot at him, but where else could he go?

He grabbed the ladder and started scrambling upwards.

He tripped.

Big Mike tripped.

He was just getting ready to fire off a shot that would hit the priest right at the base of the spine—man, was that little bastard a clean target there on that ladder—and then he went and tripped.

More hymnbooks.

Bastards.

Why'd they have to go and leave 'em all over the floor anyway?

Bastards.

He made it.

The belfry.

He stood a moment catching his breath.

In the starlight he could see the shape of the bell.

He could also see, through one of the long, wide openings in the stone, the long sheer drop to the ground.

Every once in a while the monsignor asked Father Michaels to ring the bell on holy days. Father Michaels was too ashamed to admit how afraid he was of heights, and in particular how afraid he was of this particular belfry, with all the openings through which a person could fall.

There.

On the stairs.

Wood creaking.

Breath in ragged gasps.

Big Mike.

Father Michaels looked around frantically.

Where was he going to hide this time?

• • •

Big Mike decided there might be a hatch door that the priest could close, keeping Big Mike from the belfry.

So Big Mike took precautionary measures.

He started firing one bullet after another straight up into the belfry.

He could hear them clanging off the sides of the massive bell.

He could hear Father Michaels whimpering.

Big Mike smiled.

This was probably as close as that little sissy shit had ever gotten to gunfire.

Well, son, how do you like it?

Scary, ain't it?

Real scary.

He squeezed off some more shots.


The ricocheting bullets sent the priest to the lone dark corner that was not close to one of the openings.

He huddled there, knees and teeth chattering. He almost smiled. He'd long thought that the chattering thing was nonsense, made up by people who liked to tell a good story. But no. It was true.

As he huddled in the darkness, his knees and teeth made more noise than Big Mike's breathing.


Darkness.

That was all Big Mike saw when he first reached the belfry.

There was the shape of the massive bell in the starlight but nothing else.

Until . . .

Until his eyes became a little more accustomed to the dark and he began to see, there in the corner no more than four feet from him, a pair of frightened eyes.

"Hi, Father. I been lookin' for you."

"I have a gun."

"Sure ya do, Father. Sure ya do."

Big Mike stepped off the ladder, onto the two-by-fours that formed the belfry floor.

"Yer huddled up there pretty good."

"This is the house of the Lord."

"Save that bullshit for Sunday mornings. What I want from you is what the Silver Stallion means."

Big Mike could hear the priest slowly standing. Slowly starting to inch away from the dark corner.

Big Mike had to smile at that one. Up here, where exactly was the priest gonna go to anyway?

Big Mike started to move.

He saw now what the priest was trying to do.

Get closer to the ladder.

Maybe luck out and get downstairs again.

Sure, Father. Sure.

Big Mike surprised the priest by switching tactics. Instead of going around the far side of the bell, thereby giving Father Michaels time to reach the ladder, Big Mike started going around the short way.

Father Michaels, unsure of what to do, froze.

Right there.

No more than a foot from Big Mike.

Froze.

And then Big Mike grabbed him.

"Now you tell me about the Silver—"

But he didn't get to finish his sentence because the priest, lost to his own panic now, tore away from Big Mike and stumbled backwards, right toward one of the long, wide openings—

Right toward—

# 39

Eve said, "Look. Up there. In the belfry."

Slocum, Lilly, and Eve were hurrying across the corner opposite the church where they would find Father Michaels, the key to finding the ledgers.

At Eve's word, Slocum and Lilly looked up.

Neither could quite believe what they saw. Through one of the openings in the belfry, a man dressed in black was just now starting to fall the long and horrifying distance to the ground.

Eve and Lilly screamed.

But that didn't help the man whose life could now be measured in seconds.

All the way down, the man screamed.

All the way down, Slocum, Eve, and Lilly watched in helpless horror.

All the way down, the thug Slocum recognized as Big Mike stood in the belfry opening, watching the priest fall to his death.

The priest came down.

And down.

And down.

He made a sound like a sack filled with laundry hitting the ground.

Except for the loud, startled whimper that followed his flesh and bones making contact with the hard dirt street, the cleric was silent.

Slocum looked up at the belfry. Big Mike had made the mistake of standing in the opening, watching the priest plunge to his death.

Slocum raised his .45, sighted carefully, then shot Big Mike in the face three times.

Big Mike now fell to the ground, making a satisfying *thwump* as he reached the dirt street.

Slocum hurried to the priest. He was surprised that the priest's eyes were still open.

Slocum gently touched the man's shoulder. "We'll get help for you, Father."

"Too . . . late," the priest said.

And obviously he was speaking the truth.

This would be Slocum's last chance.

Unseemly as it might be, he had to press the priest for the answer.

"Father . . . I need to know about the Silver Stallion."

The priest smiled.

"He was a good man, Sam was," the priest said. "And a clever one."

He then told Slocum where to find the Silver Stallion.

Slocum wanted to kick himself in the ass for being so stupid.

Of course.

He should have figured it out that first time he looked through Sam Myles's office window. It was right down there in the square.

Eve knelt next to the priest now, daubing his sweaty head with her handkerchief.

And then he died.

Quietly, simply, passed over to the next realm, the realm he had been telling others about for so many years now.

Slocum stood up. "I'll see you at Sam's office in two hours." He went over and kicked Big Mike, making sure the man was dead.

Lilly said, "I want to go with you."

Slocum shook his head. "You tell her, Eve. You be her mother and keep her here."

Eve nodded solemnly at Lilly.

"Three hours," Slocum said.

For the next two hours, Slocum raced to three different places in order to set up his trap for the mayor and his people.

Back at the whorehouse, he learned the whereabouts of the mayor . . . and the name of the banker who would help him complete the trap.

# 40

Two hours later, two hours to the exact second, two men stood in front of City Hall.

Except for a few nocturnal pigeons, the area was deserted. The fun was to be had in other quarters of the city. Not here.

The two men looked at each other. The time was here.

Each man took from his person a pistol, snugly ensconced the pistol in the appropriate hand, and then began climbing the steps.

At the top step, a guard appeared from the shadows and started to level a shotgun at the men.

Slocum shot him directly in the face.

The guard, screaming, went over backwards, his shotgun clattering to the marble steps.

"Nice shot," Detective Halliwell said.

"I was hoping for something a little more challenging," Slocum said. And grinned.

"Yeah, I guess it was a pretty easy shot at that," Detective Halliwell said. And grinned back.

Inside they went, up yet another stairway to the first floor, where yet another shotgun-toting guard stepped

THE SILVER STALLION    179

from yet another pool of shadow.

"This one is mine," said Detective Halliwell.

He shot the man twice, in the gullet and right eye.

"Show-off," Slocum said.

They continued down the wide corridor, their footsteps echoing mightily in the vast empty building.

By now, the mayor of San Francisco had heard them coming, and was drawing his own pistol and shrieking like a woman for one of his thugs to come save him.

Two thugs responded, running in deep shadows and even deeper echoes to the mayor's office on the first floor.

Slocum and Halliwell saw them coming.

"Shall we?" said Halliwell.

"Why not?" Slocum said.

There was a frenzy of buckshot and noise and smoke, just as there was a frenzy of blood and screaming and quick dark death.

And then there was silence again.

And Slocum and Halliwell were stepping over the two most recent bodies.

And opening the mayor's door.

They glimpsed the mayor, but that was about all, because just at the moment that Slocum reached the threshold, Hizzoner let go with three quick blasts, driving Slocum and Detective Halliwell back to the hall.

Fucker.

They'd had it all planned out so neat. Walk into the asshole's office. Show him the ledgers that they had taken from Sam Myles's safe deposit box in the bank that had the stallion statue out front (the bank right on the square below Sam's office), and then Detective Halliwell would put the cuffs on him and haul his miserable ass off to jail. But no.

No. The asshole—the mayor, that is—was gonna make it tough for them.

"Tell you what," Slocum shouted into the now-dark office. "If you come out with your hands up, I promise not to kill you."

"I'm the mayor of this city."

Slocum almost felt sorry for the guy. He was shrieking like a girl and sounding like every bad villain in every bad melodrama ever staged.

"Not anymore you're not," Detective Halliwell called. "We have the ledgers. I'm placing you under arrest."

Slocum sighed. "Look, asshole. I'd rather kill you, but Halliwell here seems to believe in law 'n order. He wants to be a good boy and just arrest you. So if you play along with Halliwell here, you'll live out the night. But if you don't haul your ass out of there . . ."

And then they saw him.

At first he was like a phantom.

A dapper man with a walking stick and a bowler.

Now how the hell had he gotten in here?

And what was he doing here?

"Stop!" Halliwell shouted at him.

"He's the guy who's been following me!" Slocum said.

Now Slocum saw the guy's gun. Big-ass .45.

The guy had snuck up on them silently.

Now, just as silently, he was walking into the mayor's office.

Gunfire.

Shouts.

Screams.

"Let's get in there!" Slocum said.

And they piled into the large, fancy office.

And got the lights on.

Whatever his name was, the dapper phantom with the walking stick and the bowler was a damned good shot.

He'd hit the mayor of San Francisco four times in the chest, two times in the face.

Hizzoner was sprawled all over his desk, leaking blood, feces, and life.

They got the guy to sit in a chair. He looked dazed, perhaps insane.

Slocum took his gun. The guy offered no resistance.

"How come you were following me?" Slocum asked.

And so the guy explained, his voice just as dazed as his green eyes.

His father had run against the mayor two elections ago. When it looked as if his father might offer some serious competition, the mayor trumped up some morals charges against the guy and destroyed him. The son had first followed Sam Myles and then Slocum because he knew they'd lead him to the ledgers and to destroying the mayor. He wanted the ledgers to destroy the man's reputation—and he wanted his own hand and own gun to take the mayor's life.

Poor sad bastard.

Slocum felt sorry for him.

Twenty minutes later, a handful of good cops, cops that Halliwell knew could be trusted, came charging into the room and took over. Slocum shook the detective's hand and said, "I promised I'd get back to the ladies."

"I owe you a lot."

"No, you don't. You owe me just one thing."

"And what's that?"

"An apology. I told you that my friend Sam Myles

had gone straight and you didn't believe me."

"I was wrong. Very wrong."

"Glad to hear you say that, Halliwell. I'll tell Eve and Lilly what you said."

Halliwell smiled. "And there's one more thing I owe you for too."

"What's that?"

"Introducing Chan to me. I haven't seen my wife this happy since our boy died."

# 41

Slocum took Eve and Lilly out for breakfast—Lilly eating more than Eve and Slocum put together—and when they were done, when they'd talked everything over and over and over yet again: how Sam had been vindicated, how Lilly was going to live with Eve, how Eve was going to see to it that Lilly went back to school, and how San Francisco would have the opportunity to once again have a straight government . . . after all this, they walked back to Sam's office and started looking through old letters and old photographs, and they all got a little teary and sentimental, and then there was a knock on the door and there in the doorway . . .

"Do I get to come in?"

"Mother, I thought you were leaving town," Eve said.

"I tried, kiddo. But I couldn't. I guess I really do want to be your mother."

Eve smiled. "Well, you may get more than you bargained for."

"Oh?"

Eve introduced Belle to Lilly. "She'll be living with us too."

Belle turned to Slocum. "How about you, Slocum? You want to live with us too?"

Slocum just smiled and shook his head.

He'd been a little too long in the city now. Cities basically made him crazy.

He needed some open spaces and maybe a couple days fishing for walleyes, and a long night on the prairie when all you could hear were the owls and wolves, and all you could see was the moon and the stars and the jagged silhouette of mountains against the midnight skies. . . .

"If you ladies will excuse me," Slocum said. "I think it's maybe time I pushed off."

Eve laughed. "You're just afraid we're going to trap you into settling down, Slocum. You're just a chicken."

"I sure am," Slocum said, his job done now.

He headed quick and smart for the doorway.